# Mine to Protect

## Veteran K9 Team

### Book 7

## Kameron Claire

Snuggle Whore Press, LLC

**Editor: Shay M Williams**

**Covers by SWP Covers**

**!! Formerly titled Big, Bad & Broken !!**

# Dedication

*This series is dedicated to every individual
who signs a blank check on their ass
by enlisting in the Armed Forces
to serve their country—and to the
loved ones who support them back home.*

*We are Witty, Wicked & Wild wherever we go!*

VETERAN
K9
TEAM
REPORTING
FOR DUTY

# Chapter 1
## Sylvie

"Yo, big bro! How's the sandbox?" I put on a wide smile at my brother's image via Zoom. I have my computer setup on my desk in my office / storage room. The front door of my hole-in-the-wall bar is unlocked.

Not that it matters.

I haven't had a customer all day. Something is going on because my clientele dried up two weeks ago, and I'm pretty sure I know why. With my brother deployed in a combat zone, there's no way in hell I'm going to tell him about my problems back here.

Besides, I fight my own battles. I always have, and I always will.

Our last name is Santiago, but he got the nickname Saint somewhere around ten. I was only six at the time and was known as Little Saint within our family, but my brother calls me Demon instead because—according to him—a halo would never fit with my devil horns.

I can't say he's wrong.

"Hey, Demon. How's it going?"

"Fine."

"It's also fine here." Our conversations are always stinted—the two of us talking without saying much at all. We've been estranged for a long time, even though we both try to pretend like we're not.

He pops a soda and chugs it down, belching into the camera. I know, as the annoying big brother, he saved that for me. "Quiet this time around, which means the days tick by slowly."

"Better slow and safe than fast and dead." I say the same thing we've said since before he left for the military —something our mom recited when he got his driver's license.

"I guess. What's going on there?" Saint looks off camera, narrows his eyes, and slides his finger over his throat, which means someone on the other side of the computer is giving him shit—most likely about me. Apparently, Army guys love to give their buddies a hard time about their cute, sweet little sisters back home.

Joke's on them.

I'm not sweet in the slightest.

"Nothing much. Same old, same old—day in and day out. How many more days until you come home?" I pull out a glass nail file and smooth down the rough edges of my tattered and torn nails while he talks. I'm not much of a girly girl. Never have been, despite having big boobs and a juicy booty. Thanks Mom for the feminine genes that I do near nothing with except on the rare occasions when I do.

"Fifty-six here, then another thirty to out-process and ETS. You know I'm moving to Colorado."

"So you've said." I sigh. I really don't want to have this fight again.

"And you know you're moving with me," he states, as if this is a fact, which only makes me want to dig in my heels more, but again—I'm not really in the mood to fight.

"We'll see." I frown at the daylight coming through the front door. Two dark silhouettes enter my bar, but I can't make them out from this distance, their faces hidden by shadows. Only after the door closes and they're inches from my door, do I recognize them—the Lupino brothers —and it's too late to hang up on Saint without alerting him to the trouble entering my bar.

"Sylvie." Marco Lupino stops short of my desk and crosses his arms over his chest with his feet shoulder width apart. He's trying to make himself look bigger than he is—an intimidation tactic that I'm sure works on many.

But I'm not one of them.

"What do you want?" I grumble, very aware of Saint's full attention on me via the computer.

"Who's that?" he asks.

Marco glances at his brother Merca and grins. "Better question. Who is that?"

I narrow my eyes. "It's my Army Ranger brother who can kill you with his bare hands."

"Word is your brother is overseas right now, so we're not worried about him." Merca places his hands flat on my desk and leans forward, his face over my computer screen, but outside of the camera's field of view. "Does your brother own this bar?"

"Show your fucking face, coward!" Saint barks into the computer. It doesn't matter though. They are absolutely right. He can't do shit right now, and the last thing I want is for him to be worrying about me when he needs to be focused on bringing his ass home in one piece. Almost a year ago, he had a battle buddy shot in the head, another shot in the shoulder, while on a four-man patrol.

That broke something in me, and I won't survive if it happens to him. Even if we are estranged, I still love the dumb pig.

"I've already told you lug heads. I'm the sole owner of this establishment."

"Then our business doesn't concern him, and he doesn't need to be part of this conversation." Merca shuts the lid of my computer, effectively ending our call.

Fuck! That is not going to go over well with Saint. I throw my chair back and stand up, prepared to fight to my last breath.

"I'm not selling," I say for the umpteenth time.

"We've dried up your business. Your customers know not to come here. Why are you fighting us?"

"Why do you want it and every other acre of land around it?"

Marco and Merca exchange a look.

"Yeah, assholes. I know you bought up the surrounding farms. What I don't know is why." I tuck the glass nail file into my palm and take another step back from the desk, clearing the chair. Unfortunately, I have nowhere to run. They easily cover both sides of my desk and separate me from the door.

Merca's jaw clenches. Of the two of him, he is the scarier one—probably because there was a time I thought he was handsome. We even went out a couple times, but something about him had my inner warning alarms sounding, and I never allowed it to go further. I never slept with him, which is usually a second or third date activity for me—when I date. I figure, might as well get it out of the way early and see if we are physically compatible before wasting a lot of time getting to know each other.

But with him—something told me to not open that can of worms.

"Clever girl," Merca says.

"Too clever," Marco agrees.

Merca pushes off my desk and walks around the edge. "This doesn't have to be ugly, Sylvie. We're offering you good money to sell. Way more than this shit hole is worth."

"If it's such a shit hole, why do you want it?" I change my grip on the nail file, the motion catching Merca's eye as he clocks the weapon in my hand.

He grins. "Do you think a nail file is going to stop what's coming?"

I glance quickly at Marco, who takes a couple of steps back into the threshold of my office, blocking my exit. "I'm not fucking selling to you."

Merca tilts his head and Marco grabs the golf club I keep near the door. Next thing I hear is glass shattering. I make a dash for the door, Merca snatching me around the throat and pulling me against his chest. I swing my hand with the nail file, but he is expecting it, grabbing my wrist and turning until I have no choice but to drop my half-ass weapon. He picks me up, one arm banded around my waist, his other hand curled over my pussy like it was a bowling ball, and carries me three steps into the bar so I can witness Marco playing nine rounds on every glass surface I have.

Mirror after mirror, light fixtures, neon signs, bottles of booze I can't afford to replace without paying customers—he's destroying it all.

"You motherfuckers!" I scream, even though Merca's hand is once again wrapped around my throat.

"You know—" he hisses in my ear "—this didn't have to go this way. We went out a couple of times. I liked you. I tried to be patient—"

"This is because I didn't fuck you?" I try to kick back, which only makes him tighten his grips—both of them.

"No. Actually, you not fucking me only postponed what should have happened weeks ago. I was hoping we could have a little fun, but your time has run out, and this is your last chance. Sell and leave town because the next time we come, we're taking it all—" he runs his tongue up the side of my face and clamps down on my earlobe with his sharp teeth "—to include your sweet ass."

He flings me to the ground, which is covered with glass, and follows his brother out the door. I pant for breath and scramble to my feet, rushing to the front door and locking it behind them. Standing there, I'm almost afraid to glance around my little bar—which used to be our family bar—to survey the damage. I can't afford to replace this stuff, and yet, I'd rather die than sell to them.

I won't do it, no matter what they do to me. They'll have to buy it from the bank after the coroner has signed my death certificate, because that's the only way I'm giving it up.

My phone beeps with an incoming message—from Saint no doubt. I wonder how many I've missed? I can't get on a call with him looking like this: mascara streaked cheeks—even though I've refrained from crying actual tears up to this moment—and god only knows what my neck looks like right now.

Then my phone rings with a tone that is not Whats-App. I pull it out of my pocket to see a local number—not Saint's. "Hello?"

"Sylvie, it's Deputy Doyle. Your brother called from Afghanistan and said you were in trouble. I'm on my way now. Do I need to call for backup?"

I groan and pinch the bridge of my nose. Of course, my overprotective brother called Rizona SD in a situation where they'll be less than helpful. Beside Doyle, the rest of them have turned a blind eye to what's been going on in this town for the last few months.

Doyle—as sweet as he can be—is only one man, and one man can't save me or this town.

"I'm fine. You don't need to come."

He grumbles. "I'm coming to lay eyes on you or else your brother will have my ass when he gets home."

I sigh because that's one hundred percent fact. "Understood. See you soon."

Hanging up, I slide my phone in my pocket and go back into the storage room to grab a broom.

Why do they want my little bar and all the surrounding land? Are they building some kind of Walmart Supercenter or something? As ruthless as billion-dollar corporations are, I seriously doubt they would resort to hiring thugs to physically threaten the landowners. They're more likely to send lawyers.

Unless it's drugs.

I suppose it could be drugs.

There was a time—when the factory was open—this little town had real potential. They used to make paint here, but then realized they were contaminating the water with the chemicals and considering the only other thing going on around here is ranching, contaminated water leaching into our soil and killing cows couldn't happen.

That's when Mom got sick, and my dad lost his medical benefits. Of course, there was no Erin Brockovich for us—no giant investigation and no major payouts. Just a small settlement and then a lame-ass morning-after ghosting.

Now? Rizona is barely more than a rest stop along the interstate. We're one hundred miles from the border with no clear road access south, and almost the half-way point between El Paso and San Antonio.

I don't get it, but considering this bar is the only thing I have that ties me to my deceased parents and my brother, who until he separates from the military, endangers his life daily, I can't give it up.

And I won't.

I sweep as much glass as possible when there is a knock at the door.

"It's me," Doyle calls from the other side.

I unlock it, frowning when I see his phone up and camera turned on me, Saint's very pissed off mug glaring back at me. "What the fuck, Sylvie?"

"What? It's nothing. Just a little business dispute I'm working through." I snatch Doyle's phone and narrow my eyes at him, making sure I keep the camera lens off the mess.

"Business dispute?"

"They want to buy the bar. I don't want to sell the bar. It's that simple."

"Jesus," Doyle hisses, taking in the state of my place now that the door has closed and his eyes have adjusted to the darkness.

"Shut up," I growl, turning my attention back to Saint. "It's nothing."

"Are they low-balling you?" Saint asks. He's walking with his phone held in the air, wearing a tactical vest as is required whenever they are outside their quarters.

"No."

"Then what's the fucking problem? Sell the place and move to Spring City. I'll be there in three months."

"No," I say with less than one hundred percent confidence, which has been shaken to its core by the damage inflicted by the Lupino brothers.

"Goddammit, Demon. Why do you insist on holding onto that shithole?"

I'm so tired of having this fight and am in no position to entertain my brother right now. "You know what? Fuck you, Saint. You left us. You ran away after Mom died. Well, I'm not running, so fuck you!" I hang up on my brother and toss the phone at Doyle, who thankfully catches it. "Get out, Doyle."

"Sylvie," he says calmly.

"Get the fuck out!" I scream, stomping to the door and holding it open. "Now."

He sighs and walks outside. "I'm one phone call away."

I roll my eyes and pull the door shut in his face, locking it.

Fucking men and their damn hero complexes. Doyle might be the only cop not on whomever's payroll—certainly not the Lupino brothers, or whoever they work for—but what's he really going to do for me but help sweep up the glass?

No. The only person to help me is me.

I just need to be clever enough to figure out how to save this place... and myself.

VETERAN
K9
TEAM

REPORTING
FOR DUTY

# Chapter 2
## Karden

My phone rings beside me on the couch as I sit and watch the Rangers play their Sunday morning football game. Kiki lifts her head from my thigh, looking up at me with her big brown puppy dog eyes. How a slick, fierce Belgian Malinois can throw such a pitiful look is beyond me.

Recognizing the number, I mute my TV and answer. "Yo, Saint. Are you back?"

"Not yet, Karden." His tone tells me something is up. Shit, I hope he's not calling me to tell me another one of our brothers has died. I'm so tired of getting those calls.

"What's going on?"

"Can you take some time off work?"

"Why?"

"I need a favor. A big one."

"You got it." I don't have to hear what it is. If Saint is calling me from over seven thousand miles away, I'm dropping everything and taking care of his problem.

"My sister's in trouble, and as usual, her pigheaded ass won't tell me what it is. I'd come home, but you know if I ask, they're going to make me extend and do another rotation."

"No, man. Stay there and finish out your tour. I can take care of it." I stand up, disrupting Kiki's comfort. "What are we talking about here?"

"There are a couple of guys threatening her, wanting to buy the bar, and I think things are about to escalate. I've got a high school friend, ex-Army SP named Doyle, who is a deputy back home. He said they trashed the place, broken glass everywhere, and that a really bad element moved into town a couple months ago and started buying up all the property. Of course, my sister's holding out. She's such a fucking stubborn ass!" Saint growls.

I feel the frustration rolling off of him through the phone, like a caged animal unable to protect his home from invaders. "I got you. That's about a twelve-hour drive, right?"

"Ten to eleven."

"Kiki and I can be on the road within the hour. Send me her home address, as well as the bar's. I'll scope them out."

"Fair warning. She's not going to be happy about you being there." Saint lets out a deep sigh.

I chuckle. "What woman is happy when she sees me?"

"Not a woman, man. My little sister." I hear his unspoken sentiment loud and clear.

Hands and dick off.

"Roger that."

His voice drops and I can envision him cupping his hand over the phone. "Take Big Bertha with you. It's rural Texas, and there are a lot of rodents to kill."

Closing my eyes, I nod my understanding to the gods of war since Saint can't see me. "Bertha and all her friends. Got it."

"I'm sorry to ask you to do this." Saint pauses. "I owe you big."

"You owe me nothing, brother. What's yours is mine to protect, right?"

"Yeah, well, you haven't met the pain in the ass yet. I don't call her Demon for nothing."

Chucking, I run my fingers through my hair. "I'm sure it'll be fine. I'll call you as soon as I roll into town and set eyes on her."

"Thank you, Karden. Now I'll be able to sleep."

"Keep your head down, stay safe, and bring your ass to Colorado."

"Four more months, brother. Out." He hangs up. Two minutes later, I get two texts with addresses, and then I get the one thing guys like me don't get from big brothers like Saint—a picture of his little sister.

Fuck me—she's hot.

He was right not to let anyone lay eyes or anything else on her.

I make a quick call to Vale to settle my training schedule over the next week.

"Do you need backup?" he says, the same football

game playing on the TV in the background. The crowd cheers and Cher lets out a whoop, bringing my eyes to my muted TV at the same time the Rangers wide receiver, Devlin Frank, runs in a forty-two-yard touchdown.

"That's the game," I think as I turn off my TV and walk upstairs to my bedroom. I toss the phone down on my bed and hit the speaker so I can talk as I pull clothes out of my drawers. "Like you're in any position to leave Cher's side for twenty minutes, much less a week."

"Oh no, not me. I wasn't volunteering, but I'm sure Kemp could break free."

"I'll be fine on my own."

"I can't believe Saint gave up his sister," he says casually, but I know what he's thinking.

I grab my toiletry kit, checking to see what's inside from the last time I traveled. "It had to happen sooner or later. He fully expects her to move up here, so we'd have met eventually."

"Yeah, but unsupervised? He must really be worried."

"He's not happy. He told me to bring Bertha, if that tells you anything."

Vale goes quiet for a moment. "Are you sure you don't need backup?"

"I'm good," I huff.

He sighs. "All right. If you need anything, call. One of us will answer. And I'll divvy up your training between the four of us."

"Roger that. Thanks."

I hang up and call Janey—the owner of the Veteran

K9 Center—to let her know what's going on. She was military with the rest of us, and personally recruited each one of us as we approached our ETS dates. Hell, she's already got her hooks into Saint and he has another three months to go, but because of her, he knows where he's settling and that he has a job when he separates.

She did the same thing for me, Vale, Lincoln, and Barron—bringing all of us to Spring City over the last couple of years.

Even Hollywood and Bishop are here now, and they weren't K9 trainers. Just veterans and combat buddies who needed a place to land.

Well, Hollywood brings a hell of a lot with him, so maybe I shouldn't count him as a guy who needed a home, but the truth is he needs us just as much as we need him.

"Take all the time you need and be careful," she says, cutting our conversation short.

"Thanks."

I take ten minutes to pack a duffel bag for myself and twelve minutes to pack all of Kiki's shit. Where I travel light, she's a diva, requiring food, treats, her blanket, and bed, as well as an assortment of toys. It's hard to believe she's a highly trained killing machine.

I secure two high-powered rifles, as well as two handguns and extra ammo in the safe under my back-seat, strapping a Glock 19 to the holster on my hip. Colorado is a concealed carry state, as is Texas, so I shouldn't have any problems. Still, I hope I don't have to pull these out of their cradles. I really don't want to go down that road with whoever these assholes are down south.

I pray Saint is being melodramatic, but something tells me he's not. It's not his style.

Eleven and a half hours and four pit stops later, I'm pulling into a desolate town that has four stoplights. I drive by Saints and Sinners Roadside Bar. The lights are out and there are no cars parked outside. By all accounts, it looks deserted.

Then I follow maps into an old neighborhood full of 1960's single-level ranchers with chain link-fenced yards and dilapidated siding. Lights are on in her house and I get a glimpse of a curvy female walking from one room to another, her silhouette pulling off her t-shirt before disappearing into another room. One light goes off, another comes on, and it doesn't take a peeping Tom to understand she's removing her bra and unfastening her jeans.

"Sweet Jesus," I mutter, glancing around at the neighboring houses. If there are any horny teenagers living nearby, I'd say this is the house they jerk off to night after night.

As it is, there are no lights on in any of the neighboring homes, so maybe Saint's sister thinks it's too late to worry about creeps. I'm definitely feeling creepy right about now as blood rushes to my dick.

"Fuck." I slide my hand down my face as she turns off the bedroom light. I have two choices: sleep in my truck outside her house and risk someone calling the cops, or head back to the no-tell motel I passed off the interstate near her bar.

Kiki whimpers and paws at me.

"You need a break, huh?"

Her whimper turns into a growl as she fixates on something outside and behind my head. I put my hand on my hip at the same time a tap hits the window. I turn to look down the barrel of a 9mm pressed against the glass. Looking past it, I see Saint's sister with a determined look on her face.

I hit the button and roll down my window, putting one hand on Kiki who, with one word, would fly out of this window and take her down.

"Who the fuck are you?" Sylvie says low, keeping the muzzle pointed at my face.

"Hi Sylvie. I'm Karden. Saint sent me."

She exhales a big breath and lowers her weapon slightly. "Are you fucking kidding me right now? He sent some goon to spy on me?"

"First of all, I'm not a goon. Saint and I served together for many years, and now I'm a civilian in Spring City." I unfasten my seatbelt, and she raises her weapon. Putting my hands back up, I realize she's a lot more spooked than she's willing to admit to Saint or herself. "Please don't shoot me. That will really piss me off, and it will make my dog go bat-shit crazy."

Sylvie glances over me at Kiki. "Prove Saint sent you."

"You want to see the text messages or what?"

"Text messages work."

Slowly, I grab my phone off the cradle on the dash,

open up my messaging app, and pull up the last few texts he sent me, flashing the screen at her.

Her eyes scan them as she slowly lowers her weapon. "Fucking Saint."

"He's worried about you."

"Obviously. The whole thing only happened twelve hours ago, and if you are from Spring City, that means you were driving your happy ass here within the hour."

"Exactly." I put my hands down and pop the door. "I'm getting out of my truck now and I have a weapon strapped to my thigh. Do not fucking shoot me."

She waves her hands, the gun loose in her palm, which makes me even more nervous than when she had the muzzle painted on my face. Who the fuck taught her to handle a weapon? "Fine, fine."

I exit my truck and it feels good to stretch my legs. Kiki jumps into my seat, her head pressed against my shoulder. "Mind if my dog gets out, too?"

Sylvie stares at me for a minute before shaking her head and taking several steps back. "Is she going to bite me?"

"Not unless I tell her to." I purposefully glance at her 9mm. "I don't suppose you have a holster for that weapon?"

"Not on me." She glances up and down the street like a person super paranoid there is someone watching her, which is how—I suppose—she glommed onto me so quickly. "What is the chance you will tell Saint I'm good and then go home?"

"None."

"Another pigheaded soldier, huh?"

"Said like a stubborn ass, bratty little sister."

Shock and amusement pass over her face before she grins. "Where are you staying?"

"I haven't figured that out yet." I motion for Kiki to jump down onto the sidewalk. She immediately approaches Sylvie warily, smelling the weapon first. Hopefully, she hasn't discharged it recently, or the fresh scent of gunpowder will cause her hackles to rise.

"You can sleep in Saint's room."

"That would be fantastic. Thank you."

She tilts her head toward the house. "Come on, then. You can park your truck in the driveway next to the side door."

"Go with her." I motion to Kiki, who follows Sylvie into the house. I move my truck, purposely taking a lap up and down the street to note the vehicles parked on the sides.

If Sylvie's alert, I suppose I should be, too.

Something tells me this is worse than Saint fears.

VETERAN
K9
TEAM
REPORTING
FOR DUTY

# Chapter 3
## Sylvie

**H**oly shit!

Saint sent a beefcake to watch over me.

He must really be worried to send a guy that looks like Karden to protect little ol' me who is already thinking of ways to seduce him. No one this hot has come to this town in—well, ever.

His dog, Kiki, is up my ass until I put my 9mm down. Then she seems to relax and takes her time sniffing around my house. If she's a drug detection dog, she's going to go apeshit when she hits my bedroom where I had a few buds stashed in a box on my dresser until a couple hours ago.

I don't smoke all the time. I mean, it's not a daily habit, but I picked some up the last time I was in San Antonio and smoked what was left when I got home tonight. I was hoping it would settle my nerves, and it did, until an hour ago when the effects wore off.

Karden walks in with a duffle bag in one hand, a

backpack in the other. His chest is wide—a wall of hard, well-earned muscle—and his thighs bulge in worn jeans that hug his ass.

And that's not his only bulge.

He frowns at me while I'm checking him out. "Where am I bunking?"

I'm tempted to show him my room, but change my mind. "Right this way."

Saint has the middle bedroom in a three-bedroom house. This was our childhood home and was left to us when our father died after falling asleep at the wheel of his eighteen wheeler. Although it's only me now, I never moved into the big bedroom—the memory of my parents haunting me every time I set foot in there.

Karden looks around and sets his duffle down on the bed. "This was Saint's room, huh?"

On the wall are posters of football stars—Green Bay QB Aaron Rodgers and the Rocky Mountain Rangers QB Deacon Scott amongst a few others. "Yep. There might be a few *Hustlers* under the mattress if you get lonely later."

I giggle when Karden raises his brow. "I'm not sure I want to sleep here."

"I'm kidding. I took those out years ago. They're in my room now, if you want them." With those words, I sashay out of the room before we can lock eyes. If Saint is going to insist on being an overbearing pain in the ass from seven thousand miles away, I'm going to use what little feminine wiles I have to tease the shit out of the man he sent me. I know flirting with his friend will make

Saint crazy, and that's the only solace I have given the situation.

"Do you want a beer?" I call from the kitchen, digging two cold ones out of the bottom shelf.

"Sure."

Karden startles me by being a lot closer than I realize. I glance over my shoulder with my ass in the air to lock gazes with him. "Domestic okay?"

He drags his eyes from my ass to my face. "As long as it's cold, I don't care."

"A man my speed." I pop the tops and hand him one, taking a long deep draw off my bottle.

Karden watches me for a second and then takes a considerably smaller drink off his beer. He leans his hips against the wall and picks at the edge of the label. "Why don't you tell me what's going on?"

"Well. It's one thirty in the morning, and I have the best looking man I've ever pulled a gun on standing in my kitchen drinking with me." I grin, taking another long draw off my bottle to drain it dry. I motion to his bottle with my empty one. "Want another one?"

"I'm good, thanks."

"Suit yourself." I grab another one, exaggerating the stretch to put my ass high in the air.

I grin to myself as he takes in a deep breath and lets it out slowly behind me. "Why don't you tell me about what happened at the bar today?"

Rolling my eyes, I pop the top and toss the cap in a full bowl I keep on my countertop. "It's nothing. There are a couple of guys interested in buying my bar. I'm not interested in selling. They thought they could scare me by breaking a few glasses, but they were wrong."

"A few, huh? According to Deputy Doyle, they smashed every breakable surface in your bar and probably a couple hundred dollars' worth of booze."

"Fucking Doyle and his big mouth." I hiss and clench the bottle in my hand.

"Word is these guys have bought out a couple of minor land holders surrounding your bar and have bought easements with the larger landowners. Do you know why?"

I shake my head. "I have no idea."

"Have you seen these guys before a couple months ago?"

"No." His dog, Kiki, walks into the kitchen smacking her lips. "Can I pet her?"

"If she'll come to you." He nods.

I sit on the floor and am thrilled when she walks over to me, sniffing my face and hair, before nuzzling my chest with the top of her head. Tentatively, I run my fingers through her coarse fur. We've never had a dog, which is why I was so surprised Saint signed up to work with them in the military. Of course I've never met his dog, Luce, which I'm told is short for Lucifer.

I guess I should be flattered he named his dog after me.

"What kind of dog is this?"

"She's a Belgian Malinois."

"Was she yours in the military, too?"

"Yep." He nods his head, a small smile spreading across his lips. "She likes you."

"Otherwise she'd eat me?"

"Only if I tell her to." Karden arches his brow, and I'm thinking this is as close as he gets to flirting.

I take a long look at him, drinking him in from head to toe. Man, he is fucking fine. His jaw and cheekbones are sharp and angular, and there's a cleft in his chin, which gives him a hard and determined edge. I wonder what he looks like when he comes? I've yet to see him smile, and I can't imagine him relaxed, although he has some of the prettiest blue eyes I've ever seen with long lush eyelashes. "What's your story?"

"What do you mean?" He takes another quick drink, nursing his beer.

"I mean, my brother calls and minutes later you're driving south. Is there an irate girlfriend cursing my name right now?"

"No."

Jesus, he's a man of few words. "A boyfriend?"

"No."

I scratch Kiki behind her ears and she rolls over in my lap, her tongue lolling out of her mouth. "Then who keeps your bed warm at night?"

"You're petting her."

"Oh." I smile up at him. "So, there's nothing stopping you and I—"

"Not a chance in hell, Sylvie." Karden shakes his head but otherwise doesn't move a muscle.

I don't have a lot of options in a town this size, but no one has ever turned me down. "Why not?"

"Besides the fact that your brother would put my nuts in a vice? You've had a traumatic experience today, one you're obviously unwilling to deal with since I can smell the alcohol and marijuana on you."

Anger simmers below the surface as I glare up at him from the floor. "I'm not drunk or high."

"No, you're not, which is even more worrisome."

Gently, I push Kiki off my lap and stand up, down the last of my beer, and toss the bottle in the garbage. "There's food in the refrigerator, bottles of water in the cupboard, and extra towels in the closet next to the bathroom. If you'll excuse me, I'm going to take my drunk ass to bed."

He grabs my arm as I try to pass him. "You shouldn't be sleeping in the front room. Your shadow advertises your whereabouts to anyone watching from outside. Why don't you move into the back bedroom?"

"Why don't you mind your own fucking business?" I yank my arm out of his hand and stomp into my bedroom, slamming the door shut behind me.

Snatching my phone out of my purse, I WhatsApp Saint. "How dare you send someone to watch over me!!!"

He calls immediately, his face on my phone with bright sunlight behind him, much to my surprise. Usually there's a delay between when I text and when he can check and respond to messages. "You left me no choice."

I narrow my eyes. "No choice but to butt into my business? You didn't care before. Why do you care now?"

He sighs. "I always care about you, Demon."

"Fuck you, Saint." I choke back tears as I growl out the words.

He stares at me for a minute, saying nothing. "You don't mean that."

No, I don't mean that. If these are the last words I speak to him, I'll never forgive myself. And yet, I'm so angry I can't bring myself to take them back.

I'm mad he left me here almost ten years ago, weeks after our mother died.

I'm furious he came home to bury our father and then left again less than two weeks later.

I'm hurt he dismisses my need to hold on to the only relics we have left of our family. This house and our bar are all we have left. No, it isn't much. The bar didn't make enough to pay our bills, which is why our father took up truck driving, but still, it was ours.

And I'm embarrassed the hottie in the other room not only turned me down, but then called me on my bullshit.

I throw my phone down so the camera is staring at my ceiling. While I don't want to look my brother in the eye, I can't bring myself to hang up on him either. Not again. The fact that I did it earlier today has been eating away at my soul all day.

"Demon."

I don't respond.

He waits for a beat and says, "Sylvie."

Nope. Not answering him.

"Little Saint, talk to me," my brother urges, his voice softening considerably.

"I'm tired," I say to the universe.

"I know. It'll be over soon, I promise. Four more months and we start over."

Tears stream down my cheek. He doesn't get it. Getting out of the military doesn't equal a do-over. Our parents are still gone, their spirits trapped here forever.

And then what? We just leave them?

No way.

He might be able to do that, but I can't.

"I'm tired, Saint," I repeat. "I'm going to bed. I gave your friend and his dog your room. Hopefully, she'll piss on your bed."

He chuckles, but I know him, and it's forced. For a badass Army Ranger—or whatever he is—he's a pussy when it comes to confrontations with me. "She won't. She's a highly trained and decorated war veteran."

"Yeah, well, maybe I'll give her your old high school jersey as a chew toy," I mutter, turning off my bedroom light and sliding between the sheets.

Saint doesn't say anything until I pick up the phone, my face a shadow in the darkness.

"I love you, Sylvie. Don't give Karden too hard of a time, okay?"

"I make no promises."

"Tell me you love me, brat."

I sigh. "I love you, brat."

He smiles. "Get some sleep and I'll talk to you tomorrow."

"Twice in one week? What is it, Christmas?" We normally only talk once a week via Zoom on Sundays, with WhatsApp used for texting and emergency purposes only. If we talk more than that, we fight.

"Shut up." He shakes his head. "Sleep well."

"Night." I hang up, placing the phone face down to rest on my heart. The small amount of heat the phone puts off warms me, as if my big brother is sending me a virtual hug. I know it's stupid, but it's all I have, and I cling to the warmth it infuses into my soul as I fall asleep easily for the first time in weeks.

VETERAN
K9
TEAM
REPORTING
FOR DUTY

# Chapter 4
## Karden

$M$y phone beeps with an incoming message. "Thanks brother."

"I got you." I text back, needing nothing more to say. I heard Sylvie yelling at him, and him yelling back, so I know where his head is at right now.

Unfortunately, she's a complete mystery. She's closed off, tough as nails, and hiding behind booze and sex. I seriously doubt she would've come on to me if she wasn't uncomfortable about being vulnerable and scared in front of a stranger.

Considering the way she snuck up on me in the truck, I'd say she's fucking terrified right now—hyper vigilant and probably lacking a few weeks of sleep. I doubt my presence tonight is going to change that, but maybe over the next couple of days she'll relax, knowing she is safe with me.

I bring one of my rifles into the house, leaving the other locked up in my truck with my alarm set. Kiki and I bed down in Saint's old room, but I leave the door open. If I get any sleep tonight, I don't want her sneaking out without me attached to her hip. I'm half tempted to command Kiki to sleep at her door, just in case she gets crafty.

It's odd to me she lives in a three-bedroom house and stays in her childhood bedroom versus taking over the primary one. I don't know if it has its own bathroom, but you would think a woman would've made this house her home the first chance she got. From the looks of things, she has changed little in the way of decor over the years. This house was very much decorated by somebody in the nineties—her mother, perhaps?

Although Saint is one of my closer friends, I don't know a lot about his family. I know his mom died at the end of his senior year in high school, weeks before he left for the military. And I know his dad died in a trucking accident a couple of years ago because I remember him taking off for the funeral. As it was, I took care of his dog Luce while he was gone. We deployed after he came back, and he never really talked about it.

That's not unusual for guys like us. For instance, I never talk about the string of shit bags that came in through our house when I was a kid—half of whom tried to beat the shit out of me for looking at them funny. Nor do I talk about my time in and out of foster care, or the slew of siblings I picked up along the way. I only maintain contact with a couple of them and only because we all ended up in the Army. Griffin, who joined the Navy and ended up becoming a Navy Seal. And Kerr, who lives outside Chicago, went into some super secret spy shit while I went security and ultimately K9. We're all out now, but I haven't talked to either of them in over a year.

Maybe longer.

My mom, well, she's the kind of woman who can't be alone. She takes more shit than appropriate, just to keep a man by her side. I was always the sacrifice she was willing to make, and growing up with that knowledge definitely turned me into the man I am today.

Cold, distant, detached—I don't get close to people, ever. My brothers in arms are the closest thing I've had to family, and considering they die occasionally, I've learned to not hold them too close to my heart either.

After about ten minutes of lying in bed and hearing nothing coming from her room, I close my eyes. Kiki is pressed against my thigh. She's antsy too, feeding off of my nervous energy, but we're also exhausted after a shit night of shut eye and an impromptu day of boring driving crossing flat desert land. Not surprisingly, sleep takes hold quickly. I fall into fitful dreams full of familiar images from my imagination and my past.

Explosions, gunfire, screaming and yelling morph into disco lights and red-hued rooms with curvy bodies dancing on stage. Every image keeps me alert as my subconscious mixes war and sex, violence and passion— but what wakes me up is Kiki growling and jumping off the bed as a scream comes from the other room.

I'm on my feet, gun in hand, busting through Sylvie's door at the same time she flings herself off the bed and scrambles for presumably her gun under her mattress.

"Sylvie!" I bark, waking her from whatever bad dream she's having. Her head drops forward and body slumps with her hand trapped under her mattress.

My heart pounds in my chest as I realize the only threat right now is her pulling her 9mm on me.

Kiki approaches her, whimpering as she nuzzles her way between Sylvie's chest and the bed. Saint's sister's hand comes out gun free and slides into Kiki's fur. "What are you doing in my room?"

"You were screaming."

She shakes her head, but there's no heat in her movement. Honestly, I'd say she's exhausted. "No, I screamed because you busted into my room."

"No, sweetheart."

The memory of hearing her say 'I'm tired' echoes through my brain. How long has she been having nightmares? What trauma has she experienced that haunts her subconscious? How long has she lived in a constant state of heightened awareness? Anyone with combat experience will tell you that shit wears on you after a while.

"You want to tell me about your dream?" I say calmly, giving her an opportunity to talk that I know she won't take.

"Well, I was riding this really hot guy—"

"And that made you scream in terror?" I interrupt before she can get graphic with the details. I've already told her no once, and I'll say it again if I have to, but that doesn't mean it isn't difficult turning her down. Anyone else's little sister, any other situation, and I'd be all over Sylvie.

Physically, she's perfection. Beautiful, curvy, confident—everything I like. And I won't lie. Her bitchy persona sends blood rushing straight to my cock. I'd love to bend her over while holding on to a fistful of her hair and fuck that attitude right out of her.

Nothing would make me happier.

However, considering I like my balls intact, that can't happen.

"Well, then he told me no." She rolls her eyes and pulls herself up from the floor to sit on her bed.

"I'm sure the word is foreign to you, Sylvie, but you'll get used to it."

"Go back to sleep, Karden," she scoffs, sliding back under her sheets with her back to me. "I like to sleep in on Mondays, since the bar isn't open."

"Kiki, come," I say, my eyes going to the sheer pastel curtains hanging over her window. The sky outside is lightening with the rising sun, which means it's six, maybe seven am. There's no chance in hell I'm falling back asleep now, but I close her door and change clothes, my mind set on taking Kiki for a run.

We cruise the neighborhood and run a couple laps around the track attached to a school that services kindergarten through twelfth grade. There are a few cars in the parking lot, but something tells me this town is dying and there aren't enough kids to have separate grades. Most of the people I've passed are in their sixties or older, as if they were too poor to leave, but also rich enough that they didn't have to when the work dried up. This is a community taking its last breath, and I have to wonder why a young, vibrant, single woman like Sylvie would want to stay here.

She'd have a blast in Spring City. Small enough that it's not overwhelming with skyscrapers and big city hustle, but big enough that her dating options and nighttime activities would keep her busy and happy for years.

Not that I like the idea of her dating, but I guess I don't have much of a say in the matter.

Why wouldn't she jump at the chance to move out of here?

We sneak back into the house to find her door still closed. After feeding and watering Kiki, I pull my sweat-stained shirt over my head and grab my toiletry kit, locking myself in the bathroom. The water is hot, and the pressure is good, so I allow myself the luxury of soaking in the heat while I soap my body. Of course I'm semi-hard. I have been since I woke up from my dream. Sylvie joked she was dreaming about riding a guy, but in my dream, I was being ridden hard by a curvy woman with round full hips. While sex and violence often intermingle in my subconscious, this is more vivid than usual, and I know the inspiration is twenty feet away from me.

Fuck. I have to take care of this, I think, at the same time gripping and stroking myself like a juvenile delinquent who can't keep his shit together around a beautiful woman. But, considering I can't do anything else, this has to happen.

It takes me no time to go from semi to fully erect to on

the verge of coming, and although I try to imagine anyone other than the female sleeping nearby, I can't. Her lips are too perfect, and the vision of her on her knees taking me deep in her mouth has my balls tightening up and cum shooting out of my cock.

With my palm flat against the wall, I rest my forehead on my bicep as I shoot my load down the drain, panting as I choke down the groan threatening to slip past my lips. This is going to be a long couple of days, depending on what kind of excitement the trouble that brought me here stirs up. I'm itching to meet these guys, size them up, and figure out a game plan to get her out of trouble—something I'm thinking comes naturally to her.

Finally, I shut off the water and open the curtain, wrapping a towel around my waist. There is two days' worth of scruff on my jaw and I'm tempted to shave, but at the same time, I don't have the energy. After brushing my teeth, I realize I left my change of clothes on the bed and crack open the door to see Sylvie's door open and the smell of coffee permeating the air.

My stomach rumbles, and I'm gripping the towel to my waist only to come face to face with Sylvie before I can sneak into my room.

Her jaw drops as her eyes travel the length of my body. "Wow."

"Sorry." I try to duck into the bedroom but she steps in front of me, her arm stretched across the threshold.

Licking her lips, she shakes her head. "You have nothing to be sorry for."

I narrow my eyes. "Are you always so—"

"Forward?" She raises her brow.

"Brazen," I finish.

"Why? Is it making you uncomfortable? Do you want to leave?" She smirks.

I step into her space, my nose less than an inch from hers. Her eyes widen and the smile falls from her lips, but to her pigheaded credit, she does not back down. "So, that's what this is. You're not trying to get fucked, you're trying to send me running. Well, sweetheart, it's not going to work."

"It will." She pulls in a shaky breath. "Everyone leaves eventually."

Pushing off the doorframe, she swishes her hips in her tiny sleep shorts down the hallway and then glances over her shoulder. "How do you take your coffee? Black, I assume?"

"Black works," I rasp, my eyes following just as she wants.

"It's in the kitchen." She slams her bedroom door shut behind her.

Fuck!

Now I'm hard again and see the challenge in front of me. I don't think Saint understands the amount of resentment Sylvie has for him, but I know it's there. Protecting her isn't just about getting the men harassing her to back down, it's about convincing her she's not alone. She has a brother that loves her and if she'd be willing to leave this town, a full life ahead of her.

And I have to do all of that without dreaming about or promising her a future with me.

VETERAN
K9
TEAM
REPORTING
FOR DUTY

# Chapter 5
## Sylvie

**K**arden is smarter than I gave him credit for. I was positive that blatantly hitting on him would either put him in my bed and then ultimately on the road, or have him running for the hills. Either way, he'd be gone in record time, leaving me to take care of the Lupino brothers on my own. How I'm going to do that I still haven't figured out, but I see no reason to drag someone else into my problems.

I'm not the type of person to pull other people onto my sinking life raft.

Especially someone who will report my every move to my pain in the ass brother.

He walks into the kitchen in the same jeans from yesterday and a gray T-shirt with the Veteran K9 logo on the left pec. Kiki was already hanging out with me in the kitchen, but I haven't fed her because I have no idea what her dietary restrictions are. I mean, I assume she can eat raw meat, but what do I know?

"How are you fixed for breakfast?" Karden smooths his hand down his massive chest and pats his non-existent belly.

"Is that your way of asking me to make you a sandwich?" I raise a challenging brow and hand him a hot cup of coffee.

He takes a sip and then shakes his head. "Actually, I was thinking I'd cook for you, but I need to know what you have versus what I need to go buy at the store."

"Oh." I lean my hip against the counter and cradle my mug in my hands. "That's sweet."

"Don't tell anyone," he says dryly, and I swear this is him being playful.

"Well, actually, it's Monday and I have brunch at Ma's Diner on Mondays. If I don't show up, she gets twitchy."

"Sounds good. Am I invited?"

"Oh, hell yeah." I giggle, imagining Ma's face when she gets a look at him. "I insist."

Thirty minutes later, we're walking into Ma's and taking my usual table near the jukebox. Ma's has existed for seventy years, the woman in the kitchen taking it over from her mother forty years ago. It's one of the few restaurants left in town and the only breakfast/lunch diner with classic American dishes like meatloaf and pot roast. Half of my meals come from here, when I can afford to eat.

Karden walks in behind me with Kiki in her service vest beside him.

Missy, one of Ma's many daughters, comes up to the

table with two glasses of water, her eyes glued to Karden. "Holy hell, Sylvie. Who is this?"

"This is one of Saint's friends from the Army. He's passing through town."

"Wow." Missy blatantly stares at him with her mouth open.

Karden grins and looks down at the menu in front of him, saying nothing.

Well, hell. He smiles.

Who knew?

"We're going to need a minute, Missy," I quip, a possessive need to sit in his lap and claim him a mine spinning in my belly.

"Okay. I'll tell Ma you're here." She backs up, bumping into a chair at another table before righting herself and going through the door to the kitchen.

"So you do smile, just not for me," I grumble, flicking up the menu I don't need to block him out.

"If you want me to smile for you, start being nice," Karden says without looking me in the eye.

"I tried to be nice last night."

He pushes my menu down. "I'm not leaving, so stop trying to push me away."

"We'll see."

Thankfully, Doyle walks up at that moment, his gaze going from Karden to me and back to Karden. "You must be Saint's Army friend."

"What?" My jaw drops. "Saint told you he sent him, but he didn't tell me?"

Doyle frowns. "You hung up on him, Sylvie. What did you expect?"

The two men clasp hands, and Karden invites him to sit with us. I roll my eyes, my attention back to Missy as she approaches the table with Ma.

"Glad to see you." Ma gives me a side hug, her eyes on Karden.

Yep. He's the best eye candy this town has ever seen.

"I thought Saint was handsome, but damn," Missy mutters loud enough for all to hear.

"Ewww." I shake my head at her and look at Ma. "Can you hook us up with a couple of specials?"

I glance at Karden. "You don't have any dietary restrictions, do you?"

"Nope." He sets the menu down.

"Not a problem. What about you, Doyle?"

"Just coffee and a muffin for me, ma'am."

Ma pats my arm and then shoos Missy back toward the kitchen. Since it's ten a.m. on a Monday, the diner is mostly empty. Truckers were in and out by eight, and the lunch crowd won't be here until eleven thirty.

The special is a ham and cheese omelet smothered with white pepper and sausage gravy, a scoopful of last night's pot roast with one biscuit and one pancake on the side. It's a heart attack on a plate, as Saint likes to call it, but I love it.

It will also feed me for two to three days, which helps my nonexistent budget.

Missy brings it out to us in less than ten minutes, and I'm thrilled when Karden offers Kiki a small morsel of pot roast after tasting it himself. I guess he approves. Between bites, Karden and Doyle swap Army stories while I sit and quietly enjoy my coffee and breakfast, but my attention diverts when Merca walks into the diner, his eyes landing immediately on our table.

The look on his face is murderous as he clocks Karden. Slowly, he walks around the table without saying a word and puts his hands on the back of my chair, leaning down to hiss in my ear. "Fucking slut."

Karden and Doyle exchange a look, both pushing back from the table.

Oh shit. No, no, no.

I need to diffuse this quickly or else there will be bloodshed on Ma's dining room floor. "Can someone explain this to me? How am I the slut here? There are three men at this table. I haven't fucked Doyle—" I pat his hand because bless his heart, he's certainly tried in his sweet non-assertive way "—and I won't be fucking you." Narrowing my eyes at Merca, I point to Karden. "I've yet to fuck him despite my best moves. So what exactly about this situation makes me a slut?"

Karden's jaw flexes, his gaze glued to Merca.

I continue as if the testosterone surrounding the table isn't enough to choke on. "And even if I had fucked all three of you, how would that make me the slut? If I fuck you and you haven't given me a reason to stick around, that says a lot more about you than it does about me. Ever think of that?"

Merca chuckles, but it holds no mirth. "If you don't stick around, it's because you weren't fucked properly, but I promise you Sylvie, when I fuck you, there won't be anything left to leave."

Karden stands up. "You crossed the line, motherfucker."

Merca pushes back from me and stands to his full height, which is maybe an inch or two shorter than Karden. "You have a killer glint in your eye. Are you an Army Ranger like her brother? Maybe we should see who is a better shot?"

Merca opens his jacket to reveal a pistol.

What the fuck? I know where in the middle of deserted nothingness, but when did this turn into the Wild West?

"I don't kill men in cold blood," Karden says in a tone so low, I'm not sure I heard him correctly.

Merca's eyes go down to Karden's thigh, which is strapped. I mean, this is rural Texas. Even Ma has a gun somewhere within reach. He smirks and wraps his fingers around a lock of my hair before I can move out of the way. "That's too bad. I guess I'll need to give you a reason to pull your weapon."

"Not in my house, you don't." Ma comes out of the kitchen as if she is still in charge in this town, a giant rolling pin dusted with flour in her hand, completely oblivious to the fact that these men are talking about killing each other versus duking it out.

"Everyone needs to calm down." I stand up, throwing my napkin down on my half-eaten omelet.

"Merca." Marco walks in and shakes his head. "Not the time nor the place, brother. We're businessman, here to conduct business with the fine people of Rizona. Let's not make things nasty."

Merca's eyes stay on Karden, who has his gaze locked on him. I've never seen such a violent stare down on my life, blood and broken bones promised without uttering a word. "Right. Business. We have business to conduct, don't we, Sylvie? Maybe I'll stop by with those papers for you to sign. Maybe I'll drop by later tonight."

Karden grins, but there is nothing warm or welcoming about it. "Come on by. We'll be there."

This does not make Merca happy, his eyes narrowing as he slowly takes in Karden, the gun strapped to his thigh, and the dog primed to make a move by his side. I didn't realize how intense Kiki got when she was ready to attack. I think all Karden has to do to put her into action is flick his wrist.

"I'll see you later, Sylvie." Merca takes a couple steps back and then turns on his heel, following Marco out the front door.

"Was that them?" Karden's eyes are on the door as he rests his hand on Kiki's neck, calming her instantly, even though he is visibly wired tight.

I plop down into my chair and sigh, trying to make the entire situation seem like it's no big deal. I know it is a big deal, but it's my big deal. "Yep. Those are the guys that want to buy my bar. See? I told you. It's nothing."

Karden glances down at me with true anger flashing in his eyes. "Are you finished with your breakfast?"

"No."

"Let me restate." His jaw is so tight it strangles his

words. "You are finished. Grab a to-go container, if necessary." Karden pulls his wallet out of his back pocket and hands forty dollars to Ma. "It was nice to meet you, ma'am, but we have to go. Doyle, I'd like to talk to you outside."

Before I can say boo-hiss, Karden and Doyle walk out and leave me with Ma and Missy—all three of us staring after them, slack-jawed. I have never been handled like that before by anyone. I've never had a man tell me what I'm going to do and how I'm going to do it.

Sure, Saint tries to pull that bullshit when he's here, but considering he's only come home a couple times in the last ten years, good luck telling me what to do.

Plus, he's my brother—so it's not like I'm really going to listen to him, anyway.

But a man, practically a stranger—albeit a supremely hot and thoroughly fuckable man—handling me? Never.

Too bad it was fucking sexy, too, making all my lady bits wake up and take notice. How does that work?

I look at Ma, who looks down at me and nods with an approving smile on her lips. "I like him."

"He's not staying."

"Is he from Colorado, too?"

"Yeah, he's one of Saint's Army buddies."

She nods again. "Maybe you should go to Colorado with him?"

"Are you trying to get rid of me?"

Ma flashes me a small, sad smile. "There's nothing for you here, lil Saint."

"Not you, too." I stand up and snatch my purse, thoroughly disappointed in her. She was my mom's friend, my unofficial auntie, and I expect her to want to keep me close.

"I want what's best for you, and this dying town isn't it." She smacks my butt and pushes me toward the door. "Now go be nice to that man and let him take you out of here."

I grumble a list of obscenities I would never say to Ma's face and walk out the door. Karden and Doyle are having a heated conversation, one that dies as soon as I approach.

That's it. I have to put my foot down with this guy before he thinks he's getting one over on me.

I'm the boss of me, and if he thinks he's in charge, he has another think coming.

VETERAN
K9
TEAM
REPORTING
FOR DUTY

# Chapter 6
## Karden

"Get in the truck," I bark at Sylvie as Doyle walks away with his marching orders.

As soon as we got outside, I ripped into Deputy Doyle, quickly learning just how fucking corrupt this town is. It seems he's the only one not on the take, which means there's a target painted on his back—one made even bigger by his association with me today. He believes this is cartel related, but doesn't know for sure. All he knows is six months ago, things started happening, and when he brought it to the sheriff, he was told not to cause problems where there weren't any and to keep his nose out of it.

Why he's still here, I don't know.

Sylvie stomps her foot on the ground with her hands on her hips. "Listen up, bud. You don't talk to me like—"

I snatch her by her upper arm and drag her to the passenger side, swinging open the door and shoving her into the cab. "Get in the fucking truck."

Then I point to the floorboard between her legs and call Kiki. "Cover her."

Kiki jumps into the front cab and sits between her legs, putting her paws on Sylvie's thighs and her snout against her chest.

"What the hell is this?" Sylvie's eyes grow wide, but she's smart enough to go stiff and keep her hands down at her sides.

"This is to make sure you don't get any bright ideas," I snarl and slam the door shut, walking around the front of the cab with my eyes glued to her. I'm beyond livid right now—her refusal to take this situation seriously burning a hole in my gut.

These two assholes are looking to make a land grab, but worse, they are killers who are biding their time because they have orders from on high not to draw unnecessary attention to this town.

I know a killer when I see one, and I locked eyes with a man who has taken life.

No doubt in my mind.

What's worse—he's taken a lot more than that in his time. He wasn't trying to creep Sylvie out. He was making promises he fully intends to keep, and deep down she knows it. I could tell by the way she tensed up when he walked into the diner. Her instinct tells her to fear him, and she's right. He's not stable, yet she tries to push me away and pretend like nothing is wrong?

Yeah, that shit ends now.

I open my door at the same time she reaches for her door handle. Kiki growls and I shake my head. "Not a good idea. You make a run for it and she will take you down."

"What's your fucking problem?" She backs off on her tone as Kiki gets more intent. Kiki likes her, but she will do her job and treat Sylvie like the prisoner I've decided she is. At least until she pulls her head out of her ass and admits she needs help.

"My fucking problem?" I peel out of the parking lot and down the road toward the bar. "I need to know, Sylvie. Do you have a death wish?"

"What?" she scoffs.

My hands tighten around the steering wheel and I set my gaze straight ahead of me. Through my clenched jaw, I hiss, "Do. You. Have. A. Fucking. Death. Wish?"

Her silence coupled with her gaze out of the side window gives me my answer.

Son of a bitch, Saint! What the fuck did you drag me into?

It's hard enough to protect someone that doesn't want your protection, but someone who has an active desire to die—impossible.

I drive around the bar, front and back, checking to ensure none of the doors are ajar.

"What are we doing here?" Sylvie huffs, her head turned away from me.

"I want to see this bar worth dying for." I park and turn off the ignition, letting out a deep sigh before telling Kiki, "Rest."

Kiki moves off Sylvie's lap and opens her mouth, letting her tongue loll out, her eyes on me.

"Work is over. Now it's playtime. Right, Dad?" says her expression.

Not yet, girl. Not yet.

I jump out and open the passenger door, Kiki hopping out before Sylvie, who still refuses to look at me. She can hate me all she wants. I'm not leaving and I'm not letting her stubborn ass get raped and killed. "Come on. Give me the grand fucking tour."

She pushes past me to the front door, making parts of me harden and take notice. She can throw all the attitude she wants, it only makes me want to break her more.

We enter the dark, dingy bar and the first thing I notice is the lack of reflective surfaces. She's cleaned up some of the mess, but most of the light fixtures are broken and there's shattered glass covering many surfaces. I hold the door open, waiting for her to hit the lights, which she does over and over, to no avail.

"Is there not one working fixture left in here?"

She shakes her head. "They were working when I left yesterday."

"Can you open some curtains or windows or something and let in the natural light?"

Turning to face me, she rolls her eyes. "It's a fucking roadside bar in the middle of the desert. We blacked out all the windows to help with the midday drunk ambience."

She grabs a giant lantern off the wall and lights up a section of the bar. "The power must be out."

"Is that normal?"

"No." She tries to walk around the bar, but I grab her arm and pull her to me.

"Where are you going?"

"To the breaker box." She gripes, pulling her arm free and leaving me no choice but to let the door close.

I take in a deep frustrated breath and let it out slowly, following her.

In the utility closet, flipping the main breaker does nothing to improve the situation. There's not even a click, which makes me think the problem is external. "I'll check outside. You got a key for the front door on you?"

"Yeah, why?"

"Give it to me."

"Why?" she snaps.

Before I can stop myself, I've backed her up to the wall, pinning her in place with my chest, my hand wrapped around her throat. I use my thumb to force up her chin and put my nose to hers. "Your attitude is wearing thin, Sylvie. I know you are fully aware of the danger facing you, and your refusal to take it seriously and accept my help is pissing me off. I'll go outside and check the power while I make a phone call. Meanwhile, you will sit your pretty little ass in here behind lock and key until I decide it is time to leave."

"Who are you calling?" Her brown eyes lock onto mine, and I swear fire burns in them as she takes in a ragged breath.

Jesus, could this turn her on as much as it does me?

That's not good for either of us.

"Friends."

"Please, don't tell Saint." Her voice cracks, the first sign of fear flittering across her pretty face.

I loosen my grip, but still hold her in place. "Why are you so fucking unwilling to tell him what's going on?"

Her eyes fill with unshed tears. "He needs to stay alert and focused on what's going on over there. Otherwise, he might not be paying attention and take one to the head."

I let her go and take a small step back, pain clenching at my heart. "You're talking about Miller."

"He left a sister behind who had no one after he was gone." She drops her head, shielding her eyes from me. "I can't—I won't survive if he doesn't come home."

Charity was alone, and then Bishop came for her. Both of them believe they were heaven sent or something like that. Either way, they need each other, and I'm pretty sure Miller is thrilled—wherever he is. Still, in this moment, words escape me. I can't promise Sylvie he's coming home. We don't know that. We never know that.

I was there that day. Not on patrol with Miller, Bishop, Hollywood, and Saint, but patrolling with another team a few blocks away. Kiki and I got the guy who killed Miller and injured Bishop, but we were three minutes too late.

One hundred and eighty seconds—a fucking lifetime in a war zone.

"Hiding the truth from him and pretending like everything is okay when he knows it's not isn't going to change anything over there. You need to have a genuine conversation with your brother and air whatever shit this is out." I slide my hand down my face in frustration. "Give me the key."

She digs her keys out of her pocket and hands them to me.

"I'll be back in a couple of minutes." Taking Kiki outside with me, I walk around the property and notice a newer black SUV parked one hundred yards down a dirt road on the property behind the bar. I see no movement, nothing disturbing the tall rye grass grown and harvested as feed.

I glance at the time. There's a thirteen and a half hour difference between here and Afghanistan, so I forgo calling Saint and call my foster brother Kerr instead. Something tells me things are going to get bloody here, and I'm going to need the kind of help he and his brethren excel at.

He picks up on the second ring. "Karden?"

"Hey, man."

"Damn, it's been a while. Where are you?"

"I live in Colorado, but I'm currently down in Texas, taking care of a problem I could use some help with."

Kerr's voice changes, and I can tell he's walking from one room to the next. "What kind of help?"

I choose my words carefully, fully aware I'm on an open line as I walk back to my truck and pop open the back door, lifting the seat to unlock my gun safe. "A buddy of mine is deployed and his sister has some pests that are escalating to some next level shit."

"Texas?"

"Yeah. Some rink-a-dink town in the middle of nowhere off I-10."

"They want her property?"

"How did you know that?"

"Follows an MO." Kerr covers the phone and says something to someone on his end. "Let me make a call. We have guys in that region tapped into something big. They might have some information. Do you have a name?"

"Lupino, but I don't think these guys are more than facilitators in something bigger."

"Yeah, I'm thinking so, too. Give me ten minutes and you'll be hearing from someone named Royal."

"Thanks."

"Let's catch up soon." Kerr hangs up and I lock and load my rifle, intent on investigating the truck in the field.

"Come," I say to Kiki as we walk past the power box onto the property beyond. I'm circling the vehicle to find the engine still warm, but no signs of life. My hackles rise as my phone rings. "Hello?"

"Is this Karden?"

"Is this Royal?"

"Yeah."

"Thanks for calling."

"What town are you in?"

"Rizona, Texas."

He chuckles. "We're less than thirty minutes from there now. We'll stop by. Send me your location."

"Roger that. Thanks." One thing I love about my

Army brethren, we are men of few words, but what we do say tends to be important in the heat of the moment.

The other times, most of us are a bunch of dumbasses spewing idiocy.

Work to play but play at work and all that shit.

Sharing my location with Royal, I'm tempted to put my knife in the front tire of this vehicle. I wish I'd seen Merca and Marco leave the diner. Then I would know for sure if this is theirs.

"Anything Kiki?" She sniffs all around the vehicle but doesn't alert me to much of anything. "Let's go back."

I stop at the power box to find the lid jimmied open, the main power switch set to off. I make a move to pull it into the on position and then stop myself, my eyes going to the back door.

There are no coincidences.

I rush to the back door at the same time Sylvie screams bloody murder, my veins turning ice cold as Kiki and I bust into utter darkness. My eyes take a second to adjust, but Kiki doesn't need time as she rushes into the back room where growling and screaming—both male and female voices—commingle. I pull my handgun for close range action as a shot fires in the darkness, striking the wall near my head. The lantern is on the floor, illuminating the corner where Sylvie is crouched. She reaches out and spins the lantern to the other wall where Kiki has Merca on the ground, her jaw clenched on his wrist, his gun just out of reach.

He's screaming, but also reaching behind his back to pull something—presumably another weapon. I can't have that and put one slug into his shoulder, rendering his arm useless. Then I clear the 9mm on the floor and point my muzzle at his head.

"Good girl," I say to Kiki, who has a wicked grip on his forearm.

I glance at Sylvie huddled into a ball. "Are you hurt?" She says nothing.

"Demon! Are you shot?" Using Saint's pet name for her seems to pull her out of her stupor. She unfurls, her shirt ripped open and blood trickling from her lip. That's enough to send my blood rushing, drowning out any sound other than my own beating heart. In a rage, I haul Merca up off the floor and beat him in the head and face with the butt of my Glock.

"Stop!" Sylvie screams. "You're going to kill him!"

I grit my teeth and throw him out of the office into a cluster of tables and stools. He falls to the floor and Kiki is there, ready to cover him with a flick of my wrist.

"Cover." I smack my thigh and she's on him, sinking her teeth into his upper thigh.

He screams, trying to push her away with his one functioning arm, his wrist and hand useless. "The more you fight, the harder she thrashes, asshole." I still have my Glock pointed at his head, an overwhelming desire to shoot him coursing through my veins. I swore after I left the military I would never shoot another man unless my life was on the line, but knowing I was seconds away from being too late to stop him from violating her makes my trigger finger itch.

"What are we going to do?" Sylvie stands next to me,

but stares down at him with unwavering focus. She's a tough girl.

She's *my* tough girl.

"What do you want to do?" I growl, leaning toward killing him and getting it over with.

"If you kill him, his brother will come for blood."

"They're coming for blood, anyway," I hiss. "What the fuck do you think this was?"

Her voice breaks. "I don't know."

Only the sound of her tough exterior cracking could pull my focus from the piece of shit on the floor. Silent tears fall down her cheeks as the adrenaline rushing through her veins wanes. I grab Sylvie's hand, interlacing my fingers with hers. "You move and Kiki will shred you to the point that surgery won't be able to repair that leg. Got me?"

Merca continues to moan as Kiki keeps cover on him.

I pull Sylvie back into the office, my back leaned up against the doorframe so I can keep one eye on him and one eye on her. "You okay?"

VETERAN
K9
TEAM
REPORTING
FOR DUTY

# Chapter 7
## Sylvie

I can't stop my body from shaking despite my best attempt at coming across cool and unaffected. Karden's gaze in the dim light switches from me to Merca and back again. Only because the back door is cracked open is there enough light to see anything in the bar area or the shadows haunting his handsome face.

I can't believe this happened.

Merca came at me out of nowhere minutes after Karden and Kiki left the bar. I don't know where he was hiding to surprise me like he did—the bathroom, I suppose, outside possibly—but it took two seconds for him to turn violent, fisting my hair and throwing me over my desk. Then he was standing over me, grabbing a handful of my shirt and ripping it in the process, while hauling me to my feet before delivering a backhand to my cheek.

That stung enough to make me see stars, and honestly, I lost the ability to fight for however many seconds. He leaned his forearm into my throat, pinning me in place, while he made a move for my jeans, popping open the buttons.

He called me every name in the book before slamming me face first into the desk, his hand clasped around the back of my neck to pin me in place.

Thankfully, between me fighting back and Kiki charging in, he didn't get my pants down. Kiki jumped at the same time he gripped the butt of his gun. She pushed him off me, allowing me to slump to the floor and curl up into a ball in the corner. The muzzle flashed and for a second I thought he'd shot her—my heart sinking and my brain scrambling to direct my limbs to move, to act, to do something other than shut down.

Karden appearing in the doorway, the fear and rage twisting his features, was the only thing to snap me out of the comatose state I felt myself slipping into. I turned the lantern away from me to highlight Kiki and Merca on the opposite wall.

Earlier, Karden asked if I have a death wish.

I don't.

I don't want to die, but I also don't know how to live. I don't know how to move on and let go of the few happy moments of our childhood. Saint focuses on the bad things, which is why he left as quickly as he could. Me? I choose to focus on the few fleeting good memories, but for some reason those moments have trapped me here, and I know if I leave, I'll become as jaded about our childhood as he is.

"You okay?" Karden says, his voice low and meant only for me.

I shake my head. "No."

"I have friends on the way who will take care of this. Why don't you sit down until they come?"

Tears fall faster, and I wrap my arms around my midsection. I'm so fucking tired of being strong all the time. I'm tired of being alone and pushing everyone away. This can't be my life. I just want my family back, the way we were before my mom got sick and Saint went away.

But I can't say any of that because it would sound crazy. My mom died almost ten years ago. My father, almost three. What the fuck is my problem? Why can't I break free from their ghosts?

Karden uses one hand and pulls me into his chest, wrapping his arm around me. He rests his cheek on top of my head, the gun still gripped tight in his other hand.

"You're okay. You're okay. You're okay," he says over and over, I think for his benefit as much as my own.

I don't blubber, yet I can't stop the tears from falling, and I'm now truly tired—bone deep weary. My vulnerability is showing and I can't have that, so I push away from him and take the seat in my office, shrouded in darkness.

The light in the bar gets brighter, indicating that someone is opening the back door.

"What the fuck?" Marco growls at the same time as Karden lifts his weapon.

"Hands where I can see them."

Seconds later, two more male voices enter the bar and

I'm on my feet, trying to push past Karden to see who is entering my bar. Behind Marco are two men I don't know —both big, built, and heavily armed—one weapon pointed at Merca, the other at the back of Marco's head.

"You Karden?" one guy says.

"You Royal?" he says back, three pistols brandished and pointed to kill.

"That would be me. Are these your pests?"

"Yeah."

"They came early." The guy speaking, Royal I presume, presses his gun to Marco's head. "On your knees, Lupino. Don't make me blow your brains all over this bar."

Marco drops to his knees while I hiss, "Are these your friends?"

Karden nods. "Stay here."

"Yeah, right." I try to push past him, but he grabs my arm, pulling me into his chest.

"Will you, for once, do as you are told?" Karden searches my eyes and the look on his face breaks my last tough girl thread. "Please."

"Okay," I whisper.

"Stay behind the door, in case bullets fly. Yeah?"

"Yes."

"Good girl." Karden cups my cheeks for half a second, his features visibly softening, and then walks away, holstering his weapon as they zip tie Marco's hands behind his back. The second guy squats down to Merca's level as Karden calls Kiki off of him.

"Damn, man. That looks like it hurts." I peer around

the corner and watch as the second guy sticks his finger in what I can only assume is the bullet hole in Merca's shoulder, making my attacker scream in anguish.

"Nice shot. Straight through. Did you mean to miss all the major arteries?" he asks.

Karden shrugs. "I didn't want to kill him."

"Good work. Marksmanship skills. You need a job?"

Karden shakes his head but says nothing.

"So," Royal looks back at me, peeking around the corner. "Can we turn the lights on in here?"

Karden also looks back at me and shakes his head. "They cut the power outside, and I wasn't sure if they had anything in here rigged to explode."

Royal glances down at Kiki. "Couldn't she tell us?"

"Yeah, give me a couple of minutes." I watch as Karden and Kiki do something I've only seen on YouTube videos. The same thing Saint and Luce are trained to do, which is the whole reason I watched hours of footage in the first place. They do a quick check of the bar, looking for explosives, and when Kiki finds none, Karden goes outside and flips a switch, the lights inside coming on.

"You can come out now," Royal says at the same time Karden walks back into the bar. I make a move and then stop, looking at him for approval.

Holy shit! I've never asked for permission in my life. What has Karden done to me?

He gives me an imperceptible nod, but says nothing.

Oh... we are definitely talking about this later.

Royal offers me his hand. "Sorry you had to go

through this. My name is Royal, and this is my partner, Jayson."

At the same time, the back door swings open and Doyle walks in with a third man behind him. "The big guy is Baehr."

"Doyle? What are you doing here?" I shake my head. He's a local sheriff. He can't see what we've done here. How are we going to explain this to law enforcement? Is Karden going to go to jail for protecting me? Oh my god—this is exactly why I didn't want anyone else to get involved in my bullshit.

"I told him to come," Karden says beside me.

"Why?" I scoff, which makes Doyle frown. If I didn't know any better, I'd say my question hurt his feelings.

Royal's eyes go to my shirt and then to Karden. "The guy with the smashed-in face do that?"

I clutch my shirt closed, remembering I have extra T-shirts in my office. "Excuse me."

From my office, I can hear Royal talking. "You want to finish him for what he was about to do to your woman?"

His woman? I wait to hear Karden rebuff that claim, but he doesn't.

"Don't you need to keep him alive for questioning?" Karden retorts instead.

"I mean, we have two. I doubt one knows things the other doesn't. He could die." Royal's tone is so blasé as he talks about killing another man that a chill runs up my spine.

"I'll get back to you on that," Karden says back, his tone equally unaffected.

I pull off my tattered shirt and yank on a clean one, my shaking hands showing no signs of stopping anytime soon. Rejoining the men, I'm at a complete loss of what to do. This is a bar—do I offer them a drink?

Do I kick Merca while he's down?

Do I talk shit to Marco, who never liked me anyway?

An unfamiliar need to stuff my trembling hands into my pockets and keep my mouth shut comes over me, and for once, I listen.

"We'll take them and their vehicle with us," Royal says as he hauls Marco to his feet. Besides Merca moaning in pain, neither of them are saying anything which surprises me. To date, they've talked a lot, each word full of machismo.

"There's another vehicle parked about one hundred yards from here in the field behind us," Karden adds.

Royal and Jayson exchange a look, and then Jayson addresses me. "Need a new car?"

My jaw drops. "Don't you turn that over to the police as evidence or something?"

"What police?" Royal arches his brow.

Doyle is clearly wearing his deputy uniform and is standing right in front of us. He shakes his head. "There is no law enforcement here, Sylvie. As far as everyone is concerned, this never happened."

"Who are you guys?" I blurt out.

Royal chuckles. "Exterminators."

"Friends," Karden adds.

"So?" Jayson smiles. "I can make it untraceable in a matter of minutes."

Shaking my head, I wrap my arms around my waist again. I don't know why I'm so cold all of the sudden. "I don't want anything that was theirs."

Karden pulls me back against his chest and wraps his thick arms around me without speaking a word. His body is warm, and I melt against him without meaning to. "What happens after this?"

Royal shrugs. "We'll have a conversation with these two, bounce what we get off of them against what we have on the DiFallo and Vasquez organizations, and go from there. You won't see them again, but we can't promise two more like them won't roll into town in the next few days."

Baehr grabs Merca around the chest, dragging him toward the door. A little jostling and he screams from the pain seconds before passing out.

Jayson chuckles, clearly amused by Merca's pain and suffering, and then turns his attention to me. "This organization isn't going to give up on this location, unless they think it's too much trouble, but it seems like you only have one deputy who gives a shit around here, and that's not enough."

Royal glances around real quick and bumps fists with Karden. "You have my number if you need us. Unfortunately, home base is eight hours away."

"I don't plan on us being here for much longer." Karden says, his deep voice rumbling in his chest.

I open my mouth to protest, but he slaps his palm over my lips, and pulls me even tighter against his chest.

Royal chuckles, his eyes going from me, then back to Karden. "It was nice meeting you. Tell Kerr I said hey."

Just like that—three big, badass strangers walk out with their two prisoners and are gone.

Much to my dismay, Karden releases me to take a seat on a stool he picks up off the floor.

I glance between him and Doyle. "So, that's it? It's over?"

Karden and Doyle shake their heads. "No, it's not over. As a matter of fact, it's just beginning. Once the puppet masters realize that Merca and Marco have been taken out, they're going to send in their next level enforcers."

Doyle nods. "It's like Jayson said. We have no entity here in town to stand up to them. Therefore, this town is forfeit. Unless the Feds come in—which maybe they will—it's not safe here for you or anyone else who stands in their way."

"You know what that means—" Karden looks at Doyle, who nods his understanding.

"I was talking to Baehr outside, and he said if I don't have a target painted on me already, there will be one now."

"They're hiring cops all over the country. Get the fuck out of here, Doyle," Karden states matter-of-factly.

"Yeah, that's what I'm thinking."

I shake my head. "You could leave here just like that?"

Doyle shrugs. "I've done it before and I don't see any reason I can't do it again. There's nothing for me in this town, just like there's nothing here for you. Let's get out before we can't."

Shaking my head even harder, I dig in my heels. "No. Absolutely not."

VETERAN
K9
TEAM

REPORTING
FOR DUTY

# Chapter 8
## Karden

I've never kidnapped someone and held them against their will before, but I'm thinking that's exactly what's happening tonight.

Royal didn't say exactly, but he confirmed this is either cartel or organized crime, and has something to do with trafficking of some variety, whether it be human or drug or both. The one thing we know for sure is somebody else will come and they'll be a lot more vicious than the Lupino brothers.

I'm not here to save a town.

I'm here to save Sylvie.

And I will not fail my mission.

"Do you have somewhere to go?" I asked Doyle.

"I have a friend I visit from time to time in Oklahoma."

"Well, if you want to try Colorado, that's where Saint and I will be."

"I might do that. Thanks." Doyle looks around the

bar and then at Sylvie, a sadness crossing his face. Something tells me there is history and unrequited love here, and it causes something inside me to rumble. Fortunately, I like and feel sorry for him, so I see no need to puff up and stake my claim. "Guess I'll see you around."

He walks out the back door, leaving us alone. Everything happened so fast. I think it's only been thirty minutes since we walked into this bar. Maybe forty-five.

I glance around and wonder what items inside this shit hole have sentimental value. It would be good to grab a couple of keepsakes before we leave, but something tells me she's not going to do it willingly.

Her phone rings, and she pulls it out of her pocket, groaning when she sees the screen. "What do you want?"

"What the fuck happened to your face?" I'd know Saint's bark anywhere.

Sylvie puts her hand over her cut lip. "Nothing."

"Karden!"

"I'm here," I say, unable to see his face, but guilt gnawing at me just the same. They never should have touched her, and it's my fault she has a busted lip. "She was attacked, but it's over now and the guy isn't coming back."

Sylvie shoves her phone into my hands and stomps into the bathroom.

I sigh, watching her walk away as I turn the screen to face me. Saint is turning different shades of purple, pacing inside his connex with Luce sitting on the bed. "I knew I should've come home. I fucking knew it."

"Fuck you, Saint." I growl. "I've got this under

control. Yes, she got hit, and she got scared, and maybe now I'll get her to leave this fucking place because even though this guy is not coming back, new guys will."

"What the fuck happened?"

I shake my head and give him a look that speaks volumes. "It's not something I can get into over the phone, but I promise to tell you the full story when you get your ass to Colorado. Now the bigger question—how the fuck am I supposed to get her to leave here when you couldn't?"

Saint plops down on his bed next to Luce. "Honestly, my entire plan was to drug and drive her to Colorado."

"Are you serious?" I mean, I was joking in my head about drugging her, but that was his actual plan?

"Where is she right now?"

"She's in the bathroom."

"Take me outside with you. We need to talk."

I walk outside into the bright midday sun and lean against my truck, phone in hand. "Talk."

"The only way I can get Sylvie out of there is by destroying every memory she has of our parents. Our childhoods were steaming piles of shit, and I planned my escape to the hour when I was fourteen. It was unfortunate timing that my mother died weeks before my graduation date, but I had signed the enlistment papers my junior year, and was intent on having my happy ass on a bus out of town as soon as I had a diploma in hand."

He sighs, running his hands through his hair. "I fucked up by leaving Sylvie there to fend for herself while I ran away. I know that now, but I can't do anything about it except get her out of there, too."

*She holds a lot of resentment for you.* It's on the tip of my tongue, but I leave it unsaid because he's absolutely right—there's nothing he can do about it now. Something tells me they have years of therapy in their future. That is —if either of the pigheaded siblings will go.

"Sylvie holds on to the few good memories of our parents, but the reality is when our mother wasn't sick with cancer, she was addicted to a wide assortment of drugs. She spent most of our lives high and incoherent. Our father was an alcoholic before he got laid off from the factory and long before she died. He didn't fall asleep at the wheel of an eighteen wheeler, like we tell people. He was drunk and we're lucky he didn't kill somebody other than himself. That bar?" Saint slides his hand down his face, his jaw clenched. "That fucking bar. He and his buddy bought it on a whim one day—probably drunk when they came up with the bright idea—and ran it into the ground. It has never once broken even, and it's only because he sunk every dime we didn't have into buying the building that Sylvie could keep it running after he died. The co-owner—another real fucking winner—got drunk one night, beat the shit out of his wife, shot her, and then himself. Their only living son was deployed at the time, and that is the only reason he was saved from a similar fate."

"Doyle?" I guess.

"Bingo. There is nothing good about that town, Karden. So if the vultures are swooping overhead, I say fucking let them pluck it clean." Saint closes his eyes and shakes his head.

Sylvie comes out of the bar, and fucking hell, her face looks worse in the bright sunlight.

"Shit," I hiss.

"What?" Saint asks.

"Your sister's face is bruised. Keep your shit together when she takes the phone from me," I say in a low voice.

"Are you still talking to Saint?" Sylvie asks as she approaches.

"Yeah. Here." I hand her the phone and cross my arms over my chest, waiting for the explosion.

"Okay," she says before her face is on screen. "You win, temporarily."

To my surprise, Saint keeps his voice calm. "What does that mean, Demon?"

She sighs. "It means I'm not giving up the house or the bar, but I'm willing to leave town for a little while until shit calms down."

Shit here will never calm down, but I'm not going to say that.

"Thank you, Sylvie." He pauses. "Seriously, thank you. When I get home, we can fix this."

"Yeah, sure." Sylvie rolls her eyes. "Where am I going to go?"

"You'll come to Colorado with me," I say without considering anyone's feelings on the matter. This was never a question. She's with me until Saint is home, and then until she doesn't want to be anymore. I don't know if it's the adrenaline from the shooting or what, but I know she's mine to protect.

*Mine.*

"With you?" She turns to look at me and I get a glimpse of Saint's face in the camera. He's as surprised as she is, but I don't know why. What other option do we have?

"You want a sense of family? Well, we may not be blood related, but our K9 team in Spring City is about as family as most of us get. Why do you think Saint's been selling it for months?"

"Oh, that family. Sure." Sylvie sighs, her shoulders dropping. "Well, if Saint shows up, that will be his family —not mine."

"God dammit, Demon! Why the fuck do you do that? Why do you always blow me off when I talk about the future?" Saint barks, but he's right.

She's very dismissive of him.

"Because you always say you're coming home and you never do!" she screams, tossing her phone at me, which I manage to catch. I point the camera at her while she rants, pacing a small path while her arms flail.

With Saint on the phone, I'm biding my time, but fuck, she needs the insolence to be spanked out of her.

I get it.

She's hurt.

She's scared.

But she's also a petulant fucking brat who needs to be put in her place. I can't do that without crossing the boundaries Saint laid out, but honestly, I think we're past them, anyway. He and I will have to settle up once he gets home to a safe and secure sister, new job, and new life, but I know unless we go our separate ways—which is not going to happen—I won't be able to resist my need to make Sylvie mine for much longer. A day or two, perhaps, but since everything she does calls to my dominant hand, I have no choice but to accept that she and I are going to happen.

She continues to rant. "You were supposed to do two years in the military and come home, but you didn't. You re-enlisted. Then it was six years, but you were eligible for a promotion, so you re-enlisted again. Ten years, Saint! What makes this time any different?"

I turn the phone to face me. "This conversation can happen later. What you need to know right now is that the immediate threat is handled, and we'll be rolling out of town in the next few hours."

Saint looks like hammered shit, a lifetime of guilt weighing on him. "Okay."

"I got you, brother. She's mine to look after, mine to protect, and I'm going to do just that." I make a subdued claim to see if he picks up on it.

He does, if the way he locks eyes with me through the tiny screen says anything. "As long as she's safe and happy, I'm good with whatever decisions you make. I trust you."

Nodding, I glance up at Sylvie, who continues to mutter under her breath about being treated like a child while walking in a circle. "We're going to go. I'll call you when we get to Spring City."

I hang up, slip her phone into my pocket, and walk up behind her, gripping the back of her neck. "Let's grab the essentials and get out of here."

She melts into my touch, not fighting me in the slightest, which tells me all I need to know. Sylvie is hyper-independent and has taken care of herself her whole life —if Saint's account of their childhood is accurate—and while she's used to doing it herself, subconsciously she craves what I am offering.

An opportunity to give up control.

We do a quick walk-through while she stuffs a box with paperwork and pictures from behind the bar. She keeps glancing at a neon sign near the door—one of the few ones not smashed to pieces—so I unplug it and take it down. It says Saints and Sinners in hot pink neon. "You want this?"

She nods but says nothing.

I test the front door to ensure it's locked, and then follow her outside, setting the box down on the ground. "Be right back."

Inside, I hit all the breakers and turn off the gas coming into the building. Then we secure the back door and load up the truck, everything worth saving fitting into one small box.

One small box—what the fuck was the point all these years?

"We'll go to your house, pack up a couple of boxes, and be on our way. Yeah?"

She shakes her head. "I need a shower and a nap."

Standing outside the passenger side of my truck, I

step into her space until she has no choice but to look up at me. Her cheek is badly bruised, and the obnoxious ring Merca wears cut her top and bottom lip. Part of me wishes I'd taken Royal up on his offer. I have no doubt those PsySpecOps guys have plenty of empty desert to dispose of a body.

Gently, I trace the bruise and fresh cuts on her face. "I'm sorry I didn't get to you sooner."

Tears well in her eyes and spill down her cheeks. "You have nothing to be sorry for. I thought he'd shot Kiki, and I knew you'd never forgive me if that had happened."

"It's over now and we're fine." I lean forward and press my lips to her forehead. "I'll make you a deal. We pack up and get on the road, and I'll get us a nice hotel room with a giant bathtub in Lubbock or Amarillo where we can bed down for the night. Yeah?"

"Okay." She nods, wrapping her arms around my waist. There's nothing sexual in her touch this time, nor mine, and yet I feel the need to be held, loved, and cared for radiating from her body.

"Let's go, sweetheart."

She takes a little less than an hour to pack all of her stuff and a few keepsakes from her parent's bedroom, as well as Saint's. I've left her to do what she needs to do and spent my time cleaning out her refrigerator and freezer, both of which had very little in it.

I know we're not coming back here, and deep down, I think she knows it, too.

We work in relative silence, and I'm walking back

from the curb after setting out multiple bags of garbage when she walks out with two duffle bags and a giant black garbage bag full of clothes.

"Is that everything?"

She shrugs. "I never bought myself proper luggage."

"Maybe I'll get you some for your birthday." I heft her stuff and put it in the backseat, stockpiling things behind my seat.

"I've never been anywhere outside of a weekend in San Antonio, so I've never needed a suitcase."

"You're about to get a whole new world presented to you, Sylvie. Enjoy it."

VETERAN
K9
TEAM
REPORTING
FOR DUTY

# Chapter 9
## Sylvie

Hot tears press against the back of my eyeballs, but honestly, I'm all cried out so I have no idea where they are coming from. I've never had this many visceral reactions to the trauma in my life.

I thought I was tough, damn near bullet-proof, but Merca showed me how ineffectual my DVD kickboxing training really is. If Karden and Kiki hadn't been there, someone—probably Doyle—would have found my beaten and violated corpse in my office days from now. That's if Merca would've been nice enough to leave me there to be discovered. I suppose he could have had plans to take me into the desert and then no one would have found me— my brother never having answers to what happened to his little sister.

Karden convinces me to leave my car at the house and drive with him. Let's face it—my old Chevy is a piece of shit that barely made it to San Antonio and back a couple of times per year. It would never make the climb up the mountains into Colorado.

I stare out the passenger window as we drive out of my neighborhood and down Main Street until we're passing my bar off I-10, heading north toward Amarillo and ultimately Colorado. It's still early, the sun dipping below the mountains to the west, but I'm looking forward to sleeping a hundred hours.

Karden reaches over the console and grabs my hand, interlacing our fingers.

It feels so nice, and yet foreign at the same time. Normally, I would pull away from such an intimate and vulnerable gesture, but right now I can't. I'm too tired, emotionally drained, and his touch grounds me somehow.

He rubs his thumb over the back of my hand but says nothing. It's like he knows there are some things beyond words, and a simple touch is what I need right now.

Saint sucks at keeping his mouth shut, which is why we're always fighting. Neither one of us can let something go once we sink our teeth into it. Pigheaded, stubborn, obstinate—you name it, we are siblings born from it.

I lean my forehead against the window, watching the miles and miles of dirt and cattle fences pass us by, my eyelids growing heavy, the sound of the road under the tires lulling me to sleep.

Couldn't say how many minutes or hours later, but I open my eyes as Karden cracks open my door and unbuckles my seat belt. "Where are we?"

"Lubbock."

I smile. "Were you going to carry me?"

He shrugs. "You've been asleep for three hours. I was hoping to put you to bed without waking you."

"Now I wish I hadn't woken up."

"Because you want to be carried?" He raises his brow and offers me a smile.

Oh my, a beautiful smile from the gorgeous Karden? I can get used to craving it.

"I'm kidding. My ass is too big to be carried around." I make a move to step down.

Karden stops me, sliding his arms underneath me and swinging me into his arms. "Your ass is perfect, and if you want to be carried, all you have to do is ask."

I wrap my arms around his neck. "I've never been held in someone's arms before."

"Hmmm. That's a shame." He calls for Kiki and then kicks the doors shut, carrying me inside our first floor hotel room. We enter a nicely furnished space with two double beds. He sets me down on the one farthest from the door. "They didn't have suites with giant bathtubs, so I owe you that promise, but there is a nice shower with a bench seat to relax in, if you want."

*Are you going to carry me in there too?*

*Undress and wash me?*

*Maybe tuck me into bed afterward?*

The sexy, smarmy comments are on the tip of my tongue, but now that we're stuck together for a while, blatantly hitting on him seems wrong. The whole *I'm doing it to send you running for the hills* thing isn't going to cut it anymore, even if deep down I welcome him touching me in any way he wants.

One side of his mouth tilts up, as if he can hear the thoughts running through my mind. "I'll grab your bags."

Kiki jumps up on the second bed and lies down, her gaze focused on me.

I cast her a smile. "You saved my life today."

She lifts her head and jumps from one mattress to the other, lying beside me with her head on my thigh. I stroke her fur and count my blessings, gratitude burning in my chest. Not just to Kiki and Karden, but to Saint for sending them, and all the friends coming to our rescue with little more than a phone call. Is this what having friends and family is like? You pick up the phone and they are there for you, no matter the issue.

I mean, these guys didn't know Karden directly, which means they probably don't know Saint either. They know a guy in common, and yet they were willing to kill for me. I've never had friends or family like that.

Well, I guess Saint is like that after all. When he couldn't do it, he made sure someone who could, did.

Karden walks in with our bags, takes one look at me and Kiki cuddled up together, and sets them down. "She likes you."

"I like her, too."

"Well, that's good, because you're going to be living together for a while."

I wonder how she will feel about somebody else keeping his bed warm. I know he's attracted to me because I've caught him checking me out too many times not to be. And I know he feels protective of me, as was more than clear by today's events. I haven't always been nice to him, so I guess there's the chance he may not like me very much, and there is the real possibility he told Saint he wouldn't touch me.

What do I do about that?

"Did you want to take a shower?" He raises his brow as I sit here and stare at him while petting his dog.

"Yeah, but if you want to take one first, I can wait."

He shakes his head. "No. You go ahead. I'm going to order us food. Anything you're in the mood for?"

"Whatever you want. Although Kiki is telling me she deserves steak."

He flashes me a full-blown smile, and my panties get damp. So that's what that looks like. "Yeah, after today she deserves steak."

I nuzzle Kiki's neck. "You're going to get beef, baby cakes."

"How do you like yours?" Karden asks, pulling his phone out of his pocket.

"Medium to medium rare sounds great."

He glances up at me. "A girl after my heart. I'll order while you're in the shower."

My gaze drifts down to the mattress while my fingers trail over the pattern on the bedspread. "I have something I need to say, but the words are not coming easily."

I suck at apologies and thank yous and anything else that makes me feel vulnerable. I know this is one of the many ways I keep people at arm's length, but it's hard to change a ten-year-old habit—even when it's a bad one.

Karden crosses the room to stand in front of me. "What do you have to say?"

"Today, I mean, I don't have a death wish, and today..." I trail off.

Karden hooks his finger underneath my chin and lifts my head so I have no choice but to look him in the eye. "You're welcome."

He's going to kiss me.

He's going to kiss me.

*He's going to kiss me!*

I lick my lips in anticipation, his eyes following my tongue while he presses his lips together. He takes a step back, releasing my chin. "Shower, Sylvie. Now."

Deflated, I stand up and grab my small pink duffel bag. "If they have dessert, will you grab me one?"

Might as well eat my feelings tonight. Again.

"Chocolate?"

"Yeah."

"You got it."

I lock myself in the bathroom, which I'll admit is really nice. This is the swankiest hotel I've ever been to, and I'm betting it's some roadside location not far from the interstate. Just goes to show you how posh my life has not been up to this point.

Stripping off my clothes, I grab my shower stuff and turn on the water, waiting until the room fills with steam, and then soak under the spray, letting the stress and anxiety of the day melt away. Glancing at the wall, there are higher end shampoo and conditioner mounted than the stuff I brought with me—their lavender and sage scents infusing and calming my soul with every deep breath I take.

I feel like a new person when I step out of the shower —a giant weight lifting from my shoulders. Is it the knowledge that Merca and Marco aren't going to bust through my door ever again? Or the vacation from working in my dark, dank bar dangling in front of me? I own the building, so it's not like I have to make rent or pay a mortgage. While it will cost me thousands of dollars to fix what they broke, as well as replace the booze they smashed, I can plan out my grand re-opening while hunkering down in Spring City.

Obviously, I'll have to get a job when we get there. Fortunately, in a town that size I can get a decent job pretty easily. Maybe I can finally get medical benefits and go to a doctor when I get sick, something I haven't been able to do for years. Saint tried to get me listed as a dependent on his military benefits once, but I declined that shit. Looking back, my pride might need a fine tuning. It was stupid to refuse him, but I was too mad at him for leaving to let him think he was taking care of me from afar.

Just like I've been stockpiling all the cash he's been sending me over the years, refusing to spend a dime of it.

I know—stupid.

Someone knocks at the door at the same time I come out of the bathroom in my sleep clothes, my damp hair hanging around my shoulders. Karden's eyes trace over my body and he motions for me to stay in the bathroom, cracking the door and greeting the delivery driver on the other side. He takes the food like we're in a prison cell, not allowing me to see the person or vice versa.

"What was that about?" I ask as soon as he closes the door.

"I didn't want the driver to see you dressed like that." He sets two large bags of food down on the small table.

"Like what?"

"You barely have clothes on, Sylvie."

I look down at my sleep shorts and T-shirt. "What are you talking about? My clothes are no different from some teenage girl walking around the mall."

"Teenage girls don't have your body," he mutters, pulling containers out of the bag.

"Are you calling me fat?" I jokingly accuse, because I know he's not. He wants me, and without meaning to, I'm seducing him.

Just think if I put a little effort into it?

Rolling his eyes, he points to the chair. "Sit down and eat."

I take the seat, pulling my legs up underneath me and drawing his eyes to my bare flesh, hoping to entice him. It works, judging by the flash in his eyes and the slow intake of breath.

"What did you order for me?" I try to sound casual.

"Medium rare ribeye, baked potato, sautéed vegetables, side salad, bread, and chocolate cake." He sets them out in front of me and hands me a set of silverware before taking the seat across from me.

"This is a lot of food." My stomach growls as the aroma wafts off the steak.

He makes a quick plate for Kiki, chunks of unseasoned steak mixed with her kibble. She digs in at the same time he does, his meal a mirror image of mine. We eat in relative silence for the first few minutes, and I'm wishing I had a beer right now, but I know better than to say that out loud. He already thinks I have a problem—and maybe I do. I suppose I could spend my time in Spring City alcohol free, proving to him and to myself that I don't have to have it like my father did.

I make a good dent in my food, saving the rest for tomorrow, and lean back to pat my full belly. I kick my feet up on the mattress next to the table and lean back with a sigh.

"Happy?" Karden arches his brow as he pops another bite into his mouth.

"Food coma." I smile. "Thank you."

"You want to talk about what happened today?" He continues to stare at me as he picks at his food.

"I didn't take you as someone who likes to talk." I take a forkful of chocolate ganache from the top of the cake and suck on it, meeting his eye.

"I've had enough therapy to know that if you don't talk about the traumatic events, they fester and rot."

"You've had therapy?" My voice pitches in disbelief.

"You're surprised?"

"I thought you were as broken as me."

Karden says nothing and puts his fork down before standing abruptly. "I'm going to take a shower."

Shit! Me and my big mouth. Even when I'm not trying to be caustic, I find a way to insult people.

"Karden..."

He grabs a bag and walks into the bathroom, shutting the door behind him.

Fuck! How do I fix this?

VETERAN
K9
TEAM
REPORTING
FOR DUTY

# Chapter 10
## Karden

I t's not that I'm mad at Sylvie, but I'm thoroughly frustrated by her. She wears her hyper-independence like a badge of honor, keeping everybody out so nobody can hurt her.

I get it.

I used to be that person.

In a lot of ways, I'm still that person, but I'm trying to be better for myself and anyone in my future. She hasn't a clue how broken I am, but through the VA I'm working on my shit—not just from my time in the military, but my childhood, too. I'm far from fixed, but I understand myself better than I did a year ago.

I jump in and out of the shower quickly and stare at my reflection in the mirror, contemplating the shave I didn't perform this morning.

There's a light knock on the bathroom door. "I'm sorry. Too often my mouth runs away before my brain can catch up. I wasn't making fun of you for being in therapy. If anything, I'm impressed. It shows me that beneath that growly, frowny exterior is someone intent on growing into a well-rounded person. I'm sure I need to be in therapy myself, but that's a vulnerability I can't face right now."

I leave the door closed because she's talking, and something tells me as soon as I open it, not only will she stop using her words, I'll have her in my arms—and once I do that, it's all over.

"Please don't hate me. I know I've been pushing you away from the moment I pulled a gun on you, but I don't want a giant wall between us like I have with my brother." Her voice cracks, which kills me.

I open the door wearing a towel and nothing else, a replay of this morning. Her eyes grow wide when I reach out and thread my fingers through her hair, pulling her tight against my body, my forehead pressed to hers. "I don't hate you, Sylvie. I understand you better than you think."

"No one understands me." She tentatively puts her hands on my chest. "I don't understand me."

"You're going to have to trust me." I search her eyes, seeing heat and desire and a bit of fear staring back at me.

"Trust you with what?" she whispers.

"With all of you." I touch my lips to hers gently, focusing on avoiding the cuts and bruises on the right side, and lick along the seam, groaning when she opens her mouth and sticks her tongue out to meet mine.

It's not in my nature to be tender, but knowing she's hurt—especially when I should have prevented it—makes me go slow. I nibble on the corner of her mouth, trailing kisses along her jaw to her ear. "Do you want me, or are you going to push me away?"

"I want you," she moans, her fingers gripping my biceps.

That's what I want to hear.

"I'm going to make you mine, Sylvie." I rub three days' worth of beard against her neck as I slide my hands under her ass and lift her into my arms. "And once you're mine, I'm not letting go."

"Really?" She wraps her arms around my neck and her legs around my waist as I carry her to the bed.

I mean every word coming out of my mouth, even if I'm surprised by them. They are flowing out of me so smoothly, it's like I've been practicing them my whole life. "Yeah."

Sitting on the edge of the bed with her straddling my lap, I lean back and pull her down on top of me, running my hands over her thick curves, loving how her ass over-fills my fingers. She arches her back, grinding her pussy against the terry cloth towel wrapped around my waist.

"I'm not a gentle man. You should know that."

"You're holding back, aren't you?"

"After the day you had, I feel you need gentle."

"If you're going to make me yours, don't you think you should give me all of you?" She quirks her eyebrow, teasing and tempting me with one action. "I'm a tough girl. I can take it."

I roll her to her back without speaking a word, sliding my hands under her thin cotton shirt and pulling it up until it covers her eyes, bunching and twisting the material until her arms are pinned to her head. Hovering over her, I suck her pert nipple into my mouth, holding her t-shirt and hands above her head with one hand while sliding the other down the front of her booty shorts that barely function as underwear.

The things this woman wears. Well, if she was comfortable wearing them in front of others before me, that shit ends now. She will never dress like this for anyone other than me again.

But that's a fight for later.

She spreads her legs without being told to do so, letting my fingers slip right into the wet heat between her thighs.

"Is this for me?" I murmur against her breast.

"Yes." She arches into my touch, letting me find her clit plump and sensitive. It takes no time at all before she's writhing against my hand, chasing her orgasm. Her fingers clutch around the shirt securing her hands, and I wish this stupid headboard had a way to tether her to it.

Sliding two fingers into her hot pussy, I pull them out and bring them to my lips, moaning at her sweetness. "Fucking perfect."

Dipping into her honeypot again, I press my fingers to her mouth. "Open."

She sucks her juices off my fingers as I pull the T-shirt higher, taking off the makeshift blindfold. Looking down into her dark eyes that are almost black with need, I lean down and kiss her hard, pushing her past the whimper of pain it causes. She's tough, though, kissing me through her discomfort, meeting my passion with her own.

I twist the material of her shirt tighter and stretch her arms above her until her knuckles are touching the padded headboard. "You will keep your hands above your head, touching the fabric until I tell you otherwise. Understood?"

"God, that is so hot."

"What is?"

"You telling me what to do."

I chuckle, my gaze traveling down her stretched out body. "I'm glad you like it. It's going to happen a lot."

"And if I don't do what you tell me to do?" She takes her hands off the headboard a fraction of an inch, her brow arched.

"I'll punish you." I narrow my eyes, and she puts her knuckles back against the headboard.

"What kind of punishment?"

"That'll depend on the transgression." I leave it at that, saying nothing more as I slide her boy shorts down her long smooth legs and settle my shoulders between her thighs. "Did you eat your chocolate cake?"

"Some of it—" she looks down her chest at me, but keeps her hands above her head as directed "—but I left you a couple bites."

"I'm about to eat my dessert right now." I run my tongue from back to front of her pussy, her taste like pure honeysuckle. She's someone I can get drunk on—an addiction I'll never want to kick.

She's too young for you.

*Only by four years.*
She's your best friend's sister.
*He kind of gave me permission.*
She's traumatized and vulnerable.
*Yeah, I don't have an answer for that.*

All the reasons why I shouldn't do this run through my head, but the voices are quelled by one word roaring from my soul.

*Mine.*

I knew it the minute I stared down the muzzle of her gun. She was made for me, and there was no way in hell we weren't going to end up where we are right now. One way or another, she was meant to be underneath me as well as beside me.

I push her thighs farther apart and bury my mouth between her luscious lower lips, licking and sucking until she's bucking her hips and begging me to let her come. Having Sylvie come undone in my hands infuses me with a sense of pride specific to her, as if I know this is the last woman I'll ever pleasure, and therefore have to make sure she's out of her mind for me every time.

"Please. Can I bring my hands down?" Her whimper pleases me, the fact she's asking before doing what she wants to do because that's what I demand.

"Yes, baby."

She fumbles with the makeshift binds and flings her T-shirt over the edge of the bed, thrusting her fingers into my hair. "Fuck, that was amazing."

I kiss her thighs, rubbing my beard against her supple flesh before climbing her body to settle my weight between her splayed legs. I suckle her breasts, teasing and biting her nipples with just enough pressure to cause her an instance of pain before backing off.

Each hiss and moan escaping her lips only encourages me.

"Perfect." I murmur against her throat.

"What's perfect?" she asks, fisting my hair and pulling my head back to look her in the eye.

"You are—for me."

"You know, babe. You don't speak much, but when you do—goddamn." She grins and lifts to kiss me hard, wrapping her legs around my waist and pulling my hips forward.

"Do you want me?" I ask again.

"So badly."

"I have one requirement before this goes further." I can't believe I'm bringing this up now when all I want to do is sink balls deep inside her heat.

"What?"

"There are times you're going to be mad at me—no doubt in my mind. The two of us, together, explosive—but you don't shut down with me. We talk. We argue. Fuck, we'll wrestle until we're both too tired to fight, but you don't shut me out. Ever. Agreed?"

Her body stills underneath me as she casts her eyes down. "I don't know how to do that."

"We'll figure it out—together. All you have to do is be willing to try."

"For you, for us, I'll try."

Music to my ears.

I shift my hips forward, my cock perfectly nestled at her opening like he was seeking shelter.

She draws in a ragged breath, her eyes rolling back and fluttering closed. "Oh god."

Electricity wraps around my hips and settles in my balls as I sink into her heat. Part of me would love to fuck her hard and fast, but this feels too good to rush. I lift her knee with my forearm, spreading her wider and pushing deeper, making both of us feel good with slow, unhurried strokes.

Sylvie tosses her head back and moans, "It feels so... ahhhh."

I nuzzle her neck, pumping my hips harder as her pussy tightens around me. Making her come twice in however many minutes makes me unbelievably happy, my inner primal beast roaring in triumph. Plus, feeling her come on my cock will be fucking amazing. "You going to come for me, baby?"

"Oh god, I hope so. I think so. I'm out of my mind right now."

"Exactly where I want you to be." I bury my face into her neck, grinding against her until her cunt clamps down around me and squeezes, milking me for my cum. She explodes, crying out my name and digging her nails into my back as she splinters into a million pieces. "That's my girl. Come on my cock, baby."

"Oh, Karden." She releases beautifully, something I plan to make her do nightly. Getting her out of her head seems like a good plan, the only dose of therapy my untrained ass can administer daily. She's gushing wet as her pussy releases me, and I pump my hips a few more times before pulling out and fisting my cock, releasing my load on her belly.

We haven't talked about birth control yet, and until we do, I'm not going to make her feel trapped by putting a baby inside of her—although the idea doesn't horrify me.

Actually, the image of her swollen with my child makes me want to keep going.

Gritting my teeth, I release the last of my seed with my forehead pressed against her chest.

"You okay?" she pants.

"Yeah, you?"

"Yeah."

"I guess I should ask about the birth control situation." I glance up at her and grab the towel, wiping her belly clean.

"I'm not on any, but I guess I should be because I'm going to want to do this a lot."

I chuckle and roll to her side. "We'll get it set up in Spring City because I plan on us doing this a lot."

VETERAN
K9
TEAM
REPORTING
FOR DUTY

# Chapter 11
## Sylvie

I've never had sex like this—passionate, consuming, lasting all night long—until now.

I've never been able to keep my hands off someone or had them insatiable for me—until now.

I've never woken up to a man caressing me, his hand slipping down my belly and between my legs before I'm fully awake—until now.

My mind fuzzy with sleep, I arch back into his hard cock pressed against my ass and smile. "Good morning."

"Mmmm," he murmurs in my ear, rubbing my clit with his middle finger.

Then I smell his soapy skin. "Have you showered?"

Karden inhales slowly, nuzzling my neck. "Kiki and I have already run a couple of miles. She had her breakfast, and I took a shower. Now I'm waking you up the best way I know how."

"Is this how you're going to wake me regularly?" I smile and glance over my shoulder at him.

"Yes."

"Mmmm. And do you always get up before the crack of dawn?"

"I don't sleep much." He lifts my thigh and slides into me, forcing a moan from my lips.

"Me neither, except I slept great last night." I reach behind me and run my nails through his hair, loving the feel of his warm breath on my neck. This is definitely a great way to wake up.

I'm not exaggerating about my sleep habits. Normally, I'm up at least once per night, startled awake by one dream or another. Plus, I'm a night owl naturally and have been since I was a young teenager. I'm used to being in bed two to ten, not that I sleep those eight hours.

Karden appears to be a morning person. I'm not sure how we're going to make that work, but if he insists on waking me up this way, I can deal with it.

"Ahhh." I cry softly as my climax creeps over the edge, a calm yet full body orgasm causing my body to throb. So gentle, yet so powerful. Again, I've never done that with a partner before.

By myself—sure, but it's not the same.

"That's my girl." Karden pulls out and kisses my shoulder. "Get dressed. It's time to hit the road and I want to grab breakfast."

"Don't you want to come?" I roll over as he climbs out of the bed, his cock beautifully erect.

"I don't have to come every time." He pulls on boxer briefs and adjusts himself. "Get your beautiful ass up so we can go. I'm hungry."

Me too... but I guess I'll be eating on the road. I wonder if he can drive while I give him head?

I'm betting he can. He's a very talented man.

Eight hours later, we're pulling into a nice neighborhood with two-story houses, giant pine trees, and three-car garages. "This is where you live?"

"Yeah, but be forewarned, I'm remodeling, so part of it is in shambles."

At the same time we pull into the garage, his phone rings, reminding me I haven't charged my phone since waking up yesterday morning. I pull it out of the side pocket of the door where it sat all night, finding the battery dead.

"Yeah?" Karden says, his brow furrowing and eyes sliding my way. "I just pulled into the garage."

He sighs. "Yeah, I'll call you back."

"Who was that?"

"Vale from work. He's checking in. Speaking of which, we should call your brother and let him know we're here." Karden jumps out of the truck with Kiki hot on his tail.

"Well, my battery is dead, so we'll have to call him on your phone." I bite my lip, unbuckling my seatbelt. "What are we going to tell him about us?"

Karden shakes his head and grabs my bags from the back seat. "I'll deal with that later."

"Are you going to tell him?" I quirk my brow. Is he thinking we'll be done and over by the time Saint comes home and therefore there's no reason to tell him?

"Bare minimum, he's going to find out when he moves here and finds you sleeping in my bed."

I smile. That accounts for his thinking regarding me for the next three months at least.

Karden takes my stuff in the house, walking up the stairs to his bedroom. He sets my bags on the bed and then turns around to pull me into his arms. He kisses me sweetly and then pats my ass dismissively, motioning to the drawers in a lowboy dresser. "This is practically empty. Put your stuff away and then we'll call Saint together. Meanwhile, I'm going to call Vale back and find out what's going on."

"Okay." I watch Karden walk out, a sinking feeling growing in my belly. Something is wrong, and he's hiding it from me.

I try to tamp down the uneasiness festering inside me and give him the benefit of the doubt, but it goes against my nature. I can't allow my distrust to rear its ugly head as soon as we arrive in Colorado, and I certainly can't allow it to unleash itself on Karden. It seems impossible he wants something real with me after such a short time together—especially with how I've acted toward him— and yet, every word he says indicates this is real. Deep down I know I'm going to pull shenanigans to sabotage our hot and heavy relationship—that's who I am, for better or worse—and he knows it too, or else he wouldn't have said what he said last night.

I put my clothes away, his furniture a million times better than my stuff back home. Then I grab my phone and my charger, setting them up on the empty nightstand —as if it was waiting for me. The headboard is solid wood with stainless steel rivets mounted every twelve inches.

He wasn't joking about restraining me in the future. They are perfect for I-bolts.

Checking out the bathroom, I'm overwhelmed with how nice his house is. I can't imagine what he thought of my dilapidated shit hole, knowing he lives in a home like this. In the bathroom, like the bedroom, there is one side that is clearly waiting for someone else to make it their own. I take the clean sink with empty drawers on the side, putting away my hair and face stuff, toothbrushes and toothpaste, noting that his stuff is neatly stacked in the other corner. The shower, which is big enough for two, is also tidy and neat, proving that Karden is a man of few possessions, but those that he has are nice.

Once I have everything put away—I think it took me all of ten minutes, which speaks to the few possessions I own—my phone beeps with incoming messages as it gains enough of a charge to connect to the network.

I grab my cell, surprised to find five missed calls, four voicemails and six text messages all saying the same canned, official looking message. "Please contact the Crockett County Sheriff's Department immediately."

The text messages make my blood run cold. What if the unthinkable has happened and I'm finally getting the phone call I've always feared? Although, wouldn't the US Government or Department of the Army be calling me instead of the sheriff's department if something happened to Saint? What if this has to do with Merca and Marco instead? Were their bodies discovered in the desert and are being traced back to me?

My hands shake as I dial the number. At the same time Karden appears in the doorway, his brow furrowed as he looks at me.

The sinking feeling in my gut—it just tied itself into a pretzel.

I knew I couldn't enjoy happiness for more than a few fleeting minutes before something ruined it. This is why I never let my guard down, and I let no one in.

You can't be hurt if you don't make yourself vulnerable.

Dammit.

VETERAN
K9
TEAM
REPORTING
FOR DUTY

# Chapter 12
## Karden

I take Kiki outside and call Doyle back. He answers on the first ring.

"Say again?" I prompt him without a greeting.

"Has Sylvie talked to the sheriff?"

"About what?"

"He's been calling her for the last eight hours."

"About what, Doyle?" I snap.

"Saints and Sinners burned down early this morning." He sighs. "It's gone. All of it."

"How the fuck did that happen?" I glance toward the house. She's going to be devastated, and although I had no intention of her going back there, I didn't want her to lose it like this.

"Well, we only have volunteer fire out here, but best we can tell there was a leak and maybe the place filled with gas and a pilot light on the water heater ignited?"

I close my eyes. Doyle is a terrible liar, bumbling his words like a guilty criminal testifying for the first time.

"Hmmm. That's weird, because I turned the gas off before we left the bar and killed the electricity inside the building. So your theory is not possible."

"You did?" Doyle's voice pitches.

"What the fuck did you do?" I hiss, shaking my head.

"Man, you'll have to take it up with Saint when he gets home."

"Saint put you up to this?"

He ignores my question. "The sheriff wants to question Sylvie. The less she knows, the better, but you might want to be nearby when he talks to her. I let them know I had breakfast with her and a guy from Colorado yesterday and that you were leaving for a trip up north. They won't be surprised to hear she's out of town. Do you have receipts?"

"Are you fucking kidding me?" I growl, heading back into the house. "I'll deal with you and Saint later."

I hang up on him to find Sylvie standing over her phone, staring at the screen with a confused look on her beautiful face.

"What's going on?" I ask as casually as possible. Fuck, I hate lying to her first thing. This is not how I want our relationship to start, but if she finds out Saint blew up her bar—well, she's never going to forgive him and that I cannot have.

"The sheriff has been calling me since this morning. I'm calling him now."

"Put it on speaker." I sit next to her and interlace my fingers with hers as the phone rings.

"Ms. Santiago?"

"Yes."

"This is the Crockett County Sheriff's Department. Where are you?"

"I'm in Spring City with my boyfriend." She looks up at me with enormous eyes and shrugs.

I nod and squeeze her hand.

"When did you leave Rizona?"

"Yesterday afternoon. Why, what's the problem?"

"Saints and Sinners burned to the ground this morning. I was wondering if you knew anything about that?"

"What?" Tears spill down her cheeks as she stares at the phone. "It burned down?"

"This was no random fire, miss. Your building exploded and we're lucky no one was killed in the blast. I know there was an interested party trying to buy it from you. You wouldn't know where they are, would you?"

She casts her big, watery eyes to me.

I clear my throat. "This is Karden Billings. Ms. Santiago is with me and has been since I arrived in town Sunday night. The bar was closed on Monday, like it always is. We saw the interested party you're referring to briefly at Ma's Diner on Monday around ten a.m., but after that we packed up a suitcase and took a leisurely drive north to Colorado. I have time stamped receipts for gas and hotel, as well as food, if you need them. Otherwise, what do you need from us, sheriff?" I presume he is one of the dirty cops who allowed the Lupino brothers and whomever else free range to terrorize the citizens of these dying towns within their county, and therefore, I have no tolerance for him.

"This is all for now. If we have additional questions, we'll call. We don't have the manpower to launch a full investigation, and I presume the insurance company will check for arson. Meanwhile, Ms. Santiago, I'm sure the interested parties still want to buy your land. I suggest you sell what is left and move on with your life."

Sylvie squeaks as she holds back the anger and tears.

"We'll be here if you need us." I hang up the phone, frozen in place, as she shakes off my grip and stands with her hands on her hips. She says nothing at first and then pins me with dark brown eyes full of fire. "Did you do it?"

"What?" I'm surprised she suspects me.

"You went back inside before we left. Did you sabotage my bar?"

I reach out for her, but she takes a step away and holds her hands up—which pisses me off. Shutting me out was the one thing I asked her not to do. "No, I didn't fucking sabotage your bar. I went back inside to kill the gas and electricity. Everything he said isn't possible based on what I did to protect your property."

She exhales and drops her head, bringing her hands to her face. "I can't believe it's gone."

I yank her into my arms and rest my chin on the top of her head. "I'm sorry, sweetheart."

"Do you think the Lupino brothers did this?"

"Honestly, no. I don't see them escaping Royal and his team's custody, but maybe someone else from their organization. You heard the sheriff—you have no reason not to sell now."

"Fuck them. I'm not selling." She sniffles against my chest.

I close my eyes and take in a deep breath, biting my tongue. "The bar is gone. What's there to hold on to?"

She shakes her head. "I don't know, but I can't let them win."

"It's not about winning or losing, Sylvie. It's about letting go of the past and starting your future—with me."

"And what happens when you change your mind?" she blurts out, pushing me away and wrapping her arms around her waist, shutting down completely. "What happens when you get bored with having sex with me and want me to move out? I have nothing to go home to now."

On instinct, I wrap my fingers around her throat and throw her down on the bed, pinning her with my body. I put my nose to hers and stare into her dark eyes, anger and frustration wrapping bands around my chest. "I understand you're upset, but don't fucking use this as an opportunity to dismiss my feelings for you or your feelings for me. If I hadn't been one hundred percent sure about making you mine, I wouldn't have made love to you last night. People you care about are not disposable, Sylvie. What's it going to take to get you to understand and not shut me out?"

Tears slide out of the corners of her eyes. "I want to believe you."

"I told you yesterday, you have to trust me. You have to let me love you."

She sucks in her breath. "You want to love me?"

"I already do. Do you think I'd be fighting with you if I didn't?"

Sylvie searches my eyes, trying to make sense of all of this. I can't help her because it's not like me to fall for someone so quickly, but I know what I feel, and I wouldn't fight with or for just anyone. "Karden?"

"Yeah, baby?" I relax my grip on her throat, running my fingers over her lips and into her mouth. She not only gave me road head on I-25, but she swallowed every drop like a good girl, and now that I'm focused on her mouth, my frustration is dissipating.

She sucks on my fingers until I pop them free. "I noticed your head and footboards were made for restraints."

I grin. She loves me too, even if she can't say it yet. "Yeah, it was custom made for me, but I haven't used it yet."

"Will you, with me?"

"What are you saying, baby?"

"Make love to me, Karden. Make me yours."

VETERAN
K9
TEAM
REPORTING
FOR DUTY

# Epilogue
### Sylvie - Two Months Later

## Saint's Welcome Home / DD214 Party

The last two months have been amazing. Karden doesn't take my shit, but still gives me infinite patience and attention. He matches my brand of crazy perfectly, granting me the space to work through my emotional baggage when appropriate, and getting me out of my head when I dig too deep.

I love how he gets me out of my head—being tied up equals the perfect therapy session—although he says I need to think about talking to someone, too.

Whatever on that last part.

But things have been tense for the last few weeks, ever since Saint arrived back in the country and started out-processing from the military. At first I wasn't sure he'd follow through with it, but now he's here in Spring City and bunking in Karden's—oops, *our* basement, he hates it when I don't claim this house as my home—and all the things we haven't said over the last ten years are building into an epic fight. He's only supposed to live here for a couple more weeks while waiting to close on his house three blocks away, and although that is close, it's better than downstairs.

I'm finding it harder and harder to ignore him. He clearly wants to talk about our childhoods, the bar, selling the house in Rizona—all of it—and I don't want to.

We threw him a welcome home / DD214 BBQ with all the guys from the Veteran K9 Center, most of whom are his old battle buddies. It's winding down, and I'm cleaning the kitchen for the tenth time this evening, avoiding the fire pit outside where the guys are trading stories from their deployments. I don't know why hearing the stories bothers me so badly, but I must not be the only one because Charity Miller has hung out with me quite a bit.

Her and Bishop left a few minutes ago with Logan and Tess. Barron and Betty, Linc and Brandi left ten minutes before them, with Vale and Cher being the first out the door due to the baby in Cher's belly playing the bongos. She's due anytime now. Kemp and Mari are waving goodbye from the front door when Saint walks into the kitchen.

"Hey Demon." Saint has the beginning of a buzz. I can tell by his glassy eyes and the way he glances around the room, a bit of paranoia settling in. I've only drank a couple times since moving to Spring City, tonight being one of them, and I also have a slight buzz.

Neither of us is drunk, but our inhibitions are probably lower than they ought to be, considering the two of us.

"Bro," I say, turning back to the clean sink with no dishes to focus on.

"You've been hiding in here all night. Do you not like my friends?" He leans against the counter next to me, making him impossible to ignore.

"I like *my* friends just fine. I've been hanging out with them for months."

He grins. "Good. Then why are you hiding?"

"I'm not hiding."

"Yeah, you are. You've been hiding from me since I arrived in town last week."

I roll my eyes and throw my towel down. "How can I avoid you? You live here."

I turn to walk out, but he grabs my upper arm hard, pulling me to him. "We need to hash this out, Demon."

"Not right now, we don't." I try to yank my arm out of his grasp, but he's dug in tight, bruising me with his fingertips.

Karden walks into the kitchen and barks at Saint. "Let her go."

Saint's glassy eyes go from me to Karden, and he lets go. "Back off, man. That's my sister."

Karden pulls me against his chest and wraps his arm around my waist. "Yeah, but she's my woman."

Until this moment, I wasn't sure Karden would pick me over his bond with Saint. Knowing he'll fight for me, for us, takes the edge off the anxiety I've been rocking for the last several weeks.

"We need to have a family meeting," Saint says, tipping back his beer bottle and draining the last of its contents.

"Yeah, we do," Karden answers for me. "But not tonight. Maybe you should go to Janey's for a bit."

"What?" Janey LaVey, the owner of the Veteran K9 Center, pops into the kitchen with her cooler on her shoulder and car keys in her hand.

Karden arches his brow at her downright indignation. We've talked about this in private. Everyone thinks there is history between Saint and Janey, but no one knows for sure and they aren't talking. "Just to hang out for a bit and get him out of the house."

Janey looks at her watch and sighs. "I guess it is early. Want to hit the local joint and play a round or two of pool?"

Saint has his gaze glued to me during this entire exchange. He shakes his head, disappointed in me again, and nods to Janey. "Pool sounds good."

We watch them leave, and the simple act of him walking out the front door takes a load off my shoulders, like I can breathe for the first time in a week.

"Thank you," I murmur, making a conscious effort to show Karden my gratitude when I'm feeling it.

"Sweetheart, the two of you have to talk—and soon."

"We will... when he has somewhere else to live." I extricate myself from Karden's arms and pick up the dish towel, folding it pretty.

"So you can run away?" Karden leans his hip against the counter and crosses his arms over his massive chest. Man, I hate it when he psychoanalyzes me.

"No." I roll my eyes.

Karden's jaw tightens and his eyes narrow, but he says nothing.

"There's nothing to talk about. I'm angry and I have to figure out how to get over it. That's all."

"If you talk about it, then maybe you'll be able to let go of some of the rage." Karden pushes off the counter and walks out of the kitchen, turning to face me before he walks outside. "The transition from military to civilian life is hard, Sylvie, even when you have a job and support system that understands like Saint does. Everything you're mad about—childhood trauma, his abandonment, his PTSD, your PTSD, the shit you went through by yourself, everything that feeds your hyper-independence —your brother has his own version that may or may not coincide with yours. Until the two of you work through this, there is going to be tension between the three of us— and try as I might to not allow it to affect our relationship, it does and it will. I love you, but I need you to give him the same consideration I asked of you on day one. Don't shut him out. If you can't do it for him, then do it for us."

I watch Karden walk outside, my heart feeling like it's being ripped out of my chest.

Saint was wrong to approach me during his party, but he was absolutely right when he accused me of avoiding him.

Could my unwillingness to forgive him cause the end of me and Karden?

My anger at Saint is all I have left. I can't yell at my mother for dying and leaving me to become the woman of the house. Not that she was much of a housekeeper when she was alive, but when she died, I became the de facto homemaker. Saint was gone, so there was no one to stick up for me and tell my father it wasn't right that a fourteen-year-old was running the house. I went to school, but I also cooked, cleaned, and did the grocery shopping, as well as made sure my father was up, showered, and fed each morning in time for work. While he never physically abused me, he neglected us our whole lives. I was working at the bar at fifteen, cleaning tables and floors or serving patrons when my father was too drunk to do so. I was managing the bar by eighteen, and our father died the day after my twenty-first birthday.

Forgiving Saint means I face all of that again, which I don't want to do, even though I do it nightly.

But I can't lose Karden. He's the only good thing in my life, and has been since the moment he entered it.

"Sweetheart." Karden pokes his head in the glass patio door. "Get you ass out here, sit on my lap, and tell me you love me."

I take a deep breath and let it out slowly, nodding and following him outside. That's so like him to give me a few minutes inside my own head, but not too long that I spiral.

The fire has dwindled, and the air is warm enough to sit comfortably outside under a thin fleece blanket. Karden sits in an Adirondack and pulls me into his lap. He grabs my chin and makes me look at him through the darkness. "I fucking love you, Sylvie, and I want you to be truly happy, but I don't think you can be while holding on to this anger and hate."

I lean my head against his shoulder, a rogue tear slipping out of my eye, and say nothing.

"We can't have this hanging over us when we get married and have kids."

"Kids?" I squeak. We've yet to talk about the future outside of me taking classes at the community college.

"Yes, baby. I want to marry you and have beautiful children together, but our kids deserve a clean slate from the shitty childhoods we had. Can't you understand that?"

"You want me to have your baby?" I say again.

He places his hand on my tummy. "I can't wait to see you swollen with my child. Have you not thought about it?"

I mean, sure I've thought about it, but I never dreamed he was also thinking about it. "Kind of."

"I'm in your corner one hundred percent. If you tell me there is a valid reason for never forgiving Saint, I'll back you. I'll kill him, but I will back you. But if time and talking can heal old wounds, then I need you to do that for our future."

I nod. "Time and talking can fix this. I'll stop being stubborn and give him a chance."

"Thank you, sweetheart." He slips his hand under the blanket and between my thighs, my legs parting as if on command for his demanding touch. "This was a nice BBQ. You are an amazing hostess."

"You think so?"

"I do." He kisses my neck, his fingertips brushing teasingly over my clit. I moan softly, letting him play with me, grounding me while working on sending me to the stars. "You made my house our home."

VETERAN
K9
TEAM
REPORTING
FOR DUTY

# Second Epilogue

## Sylvie - Two and a Half Years Later

"Hey Boss."

Max looks up from his paperwork with his brow arched. "Yeah?"

"Just reminding you I have next Friday and Saturday off."

"I have your shifts covered, but you never said what you are doing." Max puts his pen down and leans back, a huge, proud smile filling his face. "Could it be your college graduation?"

I bite my lip and nod. After I moved in with Karden, I took Tess's bartending job at the Last Stand Saloon. That was two years ago while also going to school full time for a radiology technician. "Yep. I'm graduating with my Associates Thursday night."

"Hot damn, Sylvie. I'm so proud of you." He smacks his hands together and jumps out of his seat. Max rounds the desk and has me in a bear hug before I can brace myself. "We all are."

"It's only an Associates." I giggle against his chest.

"It's a big deal, so don't diminish your accomplishments." He lets me go and takes a step back to reveal Denny, Corey, and Dawn, who are holding a gift bag with balloons tied to it, standing in the doorway.

She hands it to me. "We all chipped in. Troy and AnnaRose wanted to be here, but—"

"I know, babies." I giggle and peek inside the large gift bag, pulling the first of many items out. It's a sweatshirt with half a female skeleton with her hair done in a high ponytail with a flower in it, and the writing says "I've got a bone to pick with you..."

I squeeze the soft fabric to my chest. "This is amazing."

"Keep going." Dawn encourages me.

As I keep digging through the bag—pulling out a personalized pen set, coffee tumbler with radioactive symbols and skeletons on it, and lastly a scrub top with skeletons in NSFW position—Corey pipes up with, "Are you going to have a party?"

"We haven't planned one."

"I was going to say, my feelings would be hurt if you didn't invite us." Corey juts his bottom lip and then bites it in the least seductive way possible before Dawn elbows him in the ribs.

"What are you doing to celebrate?" Denny asks.

"We're going to dinner after the ceremony and then Karden and I are going to the mountains for the weekend."

Denny grins. "That sounds wonderful."

"Well, maybe we can celebrate the Wednesday after here at the bar."

I dip my head, an overwhelming sense of love and gratitude filling my chest. Never in my life did I think I'd have a man who loves me, not in spite of my overwhelming flaws, but because of them. My relationship with my brother is the best it has ever been, and we have a growing family through the VKC. I have a tight, sisterly bond with Mari, Cher, Tess, Betty, and Charity, and Janey and Brandi are the aunties I never knew I was missing. And the guys and gals here at the Last Stand treat me and each other like family, too. Even though I only work two days a week, I know if I ever needed any of them, they'd be there—no questions asked. "I would love that, Max. Now, don't you have your own babies to get home to?"

Chuckling, I shake my head and stuff my presents back into the gift bag as he holds his hands up and walks backwards to stand behind his desk. "I'll be out of here in ten minutes. Sonja says congratulations, by the way."

"Thanks guys." I clutch the bag to my chest and stuff it, plus the balloons, into my locker before I head out to the bar to start my shift. One more week, and the next phase of my life starts.

## Karden

"I can't believe I'm watching my baby sister walk across stage in a cap and gown." Saint claps his hands over his head as Sylvie Santiago's name is called over the loudspeaker.

It stings a bit to not hear Sylvie Billings reverberating through the room, but that's my fault. I wanted to propose to her over a year ago, but little misguided comments she's made about her self-worth over the last eighteen months told me she needed this before we take the next step in our relationship. So, I've put off proposing, because I didn't want her attention diverted from her schoolwork or this moment—an accomplishment that is one-hundred percent hers.

But this weekend, I'm putting a fucking ring on her finger, and if I'm damn good, a baby in her belly. In that exact order.

Forty minutes later, the rest of the graduating class has been called, and half of the students are tossing their caps in the air. It doesn't take Sylvie more than thirty seconds to find us in the crowd, and the smile on her face is worth putting aside my selfish needs and desires for as long as I have.

"Eeeekkkkk!" she squeals, flinging her arms wide and

jumping into my arms, effectively kneeing Saint in the stomach at the same time.

I can tell by the oomph coming from my left.

"Good job, sweetheart."

"Thank you, babe." She frames my face and kisses me hard and with meaning.

"For what?"

"For giving me unending encouragement and support, but mostly for loving me." She smiles and looks me in the eye.

"You don't have to thank me. It's my privilege to give you what you need when you need it." I kiss her and then whisper in her ear, "because you are mine to protect, mine to take care of."

Her legs tighten around my waist as she squeezes the breath out of me.

"Thanks for kicking me in the gut, Demon."

Sylvie chuckles and drops her legs. I set her down and take a step back, letting Saint and Janey give her congratulatory hugs. "I am so proud of you, brat."

"Thanks."

"I'm starving. We'll meet you guys at the restaurant." I slide my arm around my woman's shoulders and pull her close, navigating us through the crowd to the parking lot of the school. Opening the passenger truck door, I pull Sylvie into my arms and lay a possessive kiss on her. She melts against me, putty in my hands. It's my absolute favorite thing about her.

Well, it's in the top five, along with her taste on my tongue, the way she falls apart when she comes, and the way she greets me at the end of a long day. Coming home to her is better than anything I ever thought I would deserve, considering I bounced around the system as a kid.

"I'm really proud of you."

Sylvie wiggles against me, shimmying her chest against my stomach. "Can we skip dinner and go straight to the cabin?"

"No, sweetheart. Saint and Janey want to celebrate with us, and they'd be very disappointed if we ditched them."

She pouts. "You're right. I hate it when you're right."

"But..." I jerk my thumb over my shoulder. "I grabbed our bags and stuffed them in the back before we left the house, so right after dessert, our asses are heading up the mountain."

"Yes. I cannot wait to get you naked."

"Funny." I flop my hand down on the center console, palm up in invitation. "I was thinking the same thing."

The next morning, I wake Sylvie up with breakfast in bed.

She rolls on to her back with her arms stretched over her head, a big smile on her face. "Good morning."

"Mmmm. I hope so."

I wait until she pushes up into a seated position and presses her back against the padded headboard. "Pancakes?"

"Sweets for my sweetheart." I place the tray over her lap and then take a seat next to her, cutting a chunk of pancake drenched in syrup and offering it to her mouth.

Of course, I make sure a bit of sticky sauce dribbles on her chin, so I have no choice but to swoop down and lick it up.

We get three bites into breakfast before I'm setting the tray on the ground and pushing the blankets off her body. I spread her thighs and dip my head, running my tongue between her lower lips. After two years together, we know exactly how to drive each other crazy. But we've also learned how to tease each other, drawing out our orgasms until we are on the edge of screaming.

This morning, I want my woman on the brink of tears before I make her come. She needs to be so desperate to release that she is cursing my name.

I suck her clit into my mouth and slide two fingers inside of her. Her cunt clamps down on my digits, which tells me to back off her sensitive nub until she relaxes. Over and over again, I edge her close and then pull back until she's fisting my hair and growling. "Karden!"

"Hmmmm?"

"Why won't you let me come?"

"You need to be out of your mind for me."

"I am out of my mind for you. I have been since the day we met, you big goon."

Smirking, I bite down on her thigh to punish her for calling me goon, a loving pet name she uses whenever she's feeling sassy.

"Ouch." She pulls my hair again.

Lifting up, I reach under the bed and pull up a ring box, setting it on her lower belly.

Sylvie sucks in her breath. "What's this?"

"Sweetheart. Love of my life. The only pain in the ass I'll ever invite into my world. Will you marry me?"

She giggles and shakes her head. "You said that we were married over a year ago—common law."

I narrow my eyes because now she's being obstinate. She knows damn well why I pointed that out to her, and it was never intended to replace this moment. Something told me I should have tied her up before I did this, but I didn't listen. "I told you that when you were having one of your moments claiming I'd get tired of you and kick you out and then you'd have nowhere to go—all of which is complete nonsense. My home is your home—it's our home. And yes, we are common law married, so legally we are bound, but did you really think I wasn't going to put a ring on your finger or a baby in your belly? Sweetheart, we talked about this two years ago. You are mine, I am yours, and the only reason I'm pulling a ring out now is because I was waiting for you to graduate. You needed to have your future mapped out despite me, even though you will never be without me."

I flip up the lid to reveal the ring within. It's a white gold band with two accent swirls of rose and black gold cradling a champagne diamond. It's non-traditional, like her, and I knew she'd love it.

Sylvie bites her lip, tears coming to her eyes. "It's beautiful."

"Like you." I pull the ring out and grab her hand. "So, is that a yes?"

"Of course, it is a yes. I love you more than I love myself."

"I'd prefer you love us equally, but we'll work on that." Sliding the ring on her finger, I kiss her hand and roll onto my back, pulling her up to straddle me. "Can we stop your birth control now?"

Sylvie lifts and positions herself, sliding down slowly on my cock. She's so worked up that her inner walls spasm around me. "Eager to get our family started?"

"I've been waiting for two years to get you pregnant."

"Well, then, I guess my last pill was yesterday." She shifts her hips and rides me perfectly. I grip her hips and then slide my hands up to cup her breasts, rolling her nipples between my thumbs and fingers.

Sylvie leans forward and kisses me. Pancake syrup and her tart cherry taste intermingle on my tongue. It takes less than three minutes for her pussy to quiver, her long denied orgasm crashing over and consuming her while driving my need to come. I wrap my arms around her and pump my hips up, chasing my release while spurring on a second and then a third for her.

Just like our first night together, Sylvie responds beautifully to my touch, our bodies and hearts in tune even when our minds, mostly her mind, are fucking with our happiness.

We lay in comfortable silence. Sylvie is draped over my chest as I slide my hands up and down her back and over her lush ass. Two and a half years ago I rolled up to a shitty little town in the middle of nowhere Texas and caught a glimpse of my future.

We've fought, we've matured, we've grown, and I find myself more in love with her with every passing day.

"When do you want to get married?" Sylvie says with her cheek pressed against my chest.

"Well, sweetheart, I guess that depends on what kind of wedding you want. I'll marry you tomorrow, or we'll do a big wedding with all the bells and whistles.

"What about a backyard wedding followed by a BBQ?" She smiles as she lifts her head and looks me in the eye.

"I knew you were fucking perfect."

"You got yourself a no-frills woman, Karden."

"And I wouldn't have it any other way."

Coming next: Saint and Janey in Mine to Treasure
Check out the whole series here or flip to the next page.

Most of my books take place in Spring City, Colorado and feature cameo appearances from characters in past / present / and sometimes future books from all of my series. Check out my website for a cross-over / series map.

# Also by Kameron Claire

Want more **Witty** Tongues, **Wicked** Needs, & **Wild** Deeds?

## <u>Hollywood Lights (Pre-Order)</u>

* Billionaire Romance *

Show Time (Securing Selyne)

Money Shot

Three Shot

Martini Shot

Long Shot

## <u>Veteran K9 Team</u>

** Military Romance **

Mine to Cherish

Mine to Crave

Mine to Possess

Mine to Adore

Mine to Covet

Mine to Worship

Mine to Protect

Mine to Treasure

## Hot Nights with the Boss

** Forbidden Office / Age-Gap Romances **

Dating the Boss

Flirting with the Boss

Teasing the Boss

Tempting the Boss

## Rangers Football

** Sports Romance **

Play Action Fake

Quarterback Sneak

Personal Foul

Two-Point Conversion

Red Zone

Man to Man Coverage

## Short Story Collections and Bundles

Animal Attraction 4-Story Collection

Vegas Nights 4-Story Collection

Last Stand Saloon 4-Story Collection

Instalove Bundle

## Grayson Enterprises Series

Bedding the Boss

Enticing the Ex

Tempting the Teacher

Wedding the Widow

# Exclusives and Sneak Peeks

Get exclusive stories, updates, sneak peeks, and special content only available to subscribers...

Join our Mailing List Today!

Sign Up Here

# About the Author

USA Today Bestselling Author Kameron Claire writes stories with witty tongues, wicked needs, and wild deeds. Her books emphasize strong female leads and the protective alpha males who know how to love and support kick-ass, take-charge women. Many of her books contain military veterans, boss babes, gentle but dominant men, and goofy K9 hijinks.

Find her everywhere via linktr.ee/kameronclaire
Signed Paperbacks and discounted eBook bundles are available exclusively on her store
Subscribe to the Witty, Wicked & Wild community and read all her books online for as little as $5 a month.